THE ADVENTURE OF THE MISSING DANCING GIRL

THE ADVENTURE OF THE MISSING DANCING GIRL

SUNILA GUPTE

PENGUIN BOOKS

An imprint of Penguin Random House

PENGUIN BOOKS

USA | Canada | UK | Ireland | Australia
New Zealand | India | South Africa | China | Singapore

Penguin Books is part of the Penguin Random House group of companies whose addresses can be found at global.penguinrandomhouse.com

Published by Penguin Random House India Pvt. Ltd
4th Floor, Capital Tower 1, MG Road,
Gurugram 122 002, Haryana, India

Penguin Random House India

First published by Random House India 2009

This edition published in Penguin Books by Penguin Random House India 2020

10 9 8 7 6 5 4 3 2

ISBN 9788184000634

Typeset by Inosoft Systems
Printed at Repro India Limited

www.penguin.co.in

MIX
Paper from responsible sources
FSC® C047271
FSC www.fsc.org

This is a legitimate digitally printed version of the book and therefore might not have certain extra finishing on the cover.

For Niteen,
and also
for Priya

Contents

Stowaway	1
Wild boar! A hair-raising rescue	12
Harappan times, 2500 BC: The journey begins	20
Joker… and an elephant ride!	34
Atop Champakali	40
Lothal at last!	49
Lothal dockyard	60
The great house of grain and goods and trade	67
Amu's story	71
Hiding the scroll	84
Things happen	95
Where is Namami?	99
What had happened to Namami?	107
Freedom	112
Joker is smart	116
Xerxes and Kartik wait for Appa	123

All together again	131
What Xerxes overhears!	141
The meeting	148
The lower town and the artisans	155
The white parrot	164
The priest-king's prophecy	170
Treachery	174
Captive	182
Appa finally arrives	187
Action	193
The secret of the map	197
A Trap is laid	207
Sohrab's story	225
Surya Mela	233

Amu's voyage from Mesopotamia to Meluhha
The city of the Surya Mela
MESOPOTAMIA
Kish
Nippur
River Tigris
River Euphrates
Umma
Lagash
Ur
PERSIA
Gulf of Persia
Dilmun
ARABIA

AMU'S JOURNEY

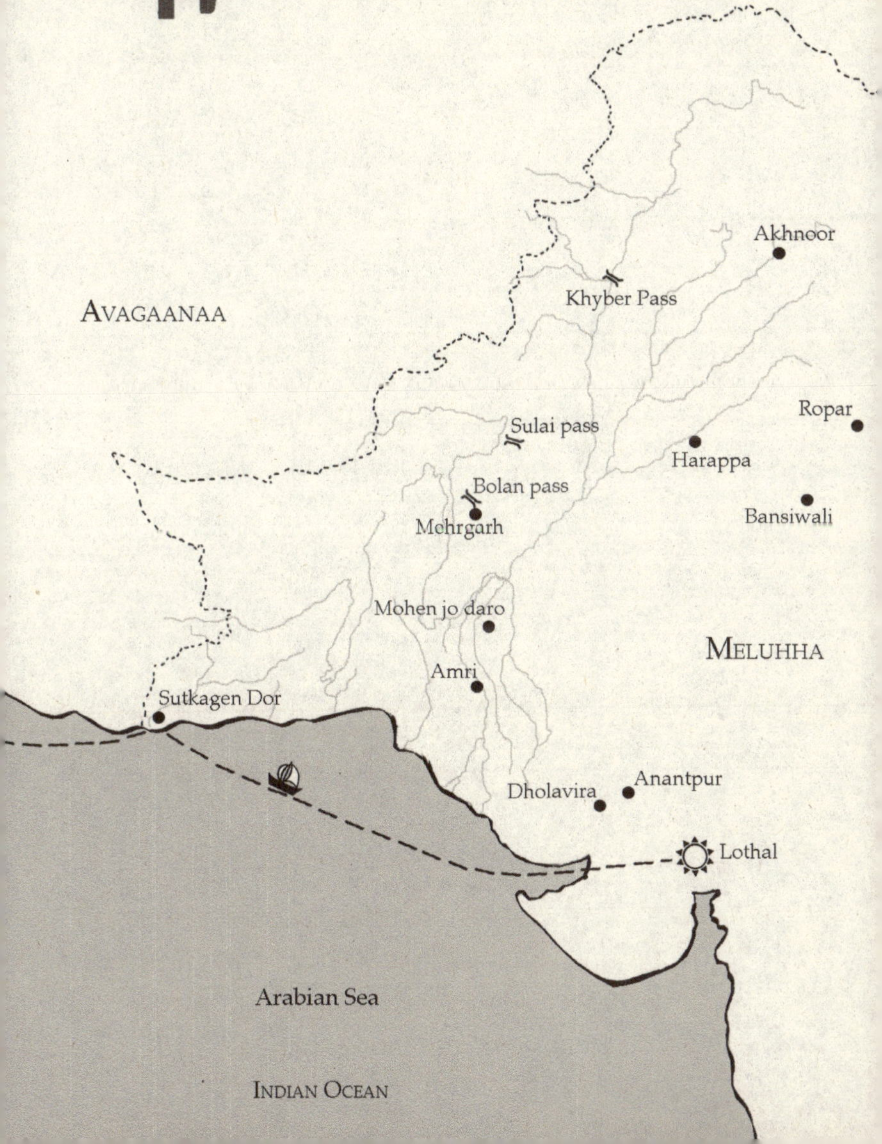

Stowaway

Amu Darya, also known as Amu, looked around furtively. He was hiding, aboard a large sailing ship, and had to make sure he stayed out of sight; more and more difficult as the hours went by. But at least they were well on their way, the tide giving them that extra push.

'Hey, you! What are you doing here?' shouted a loud voice, raised in anger. 'A stowaway, are you? I'll show you what happens to boys who hide in boats!' Amu was pulled up roughly by a sailor. He ducked quickly, dodging the clip he would have got on his ear.

He had had a difficult time, keeping out of sight, sliding between bales of cloth, sacks of bitumen, and various types of cargo; lying motionless under the camel leather covers; switching hiding places as quietly as possible. Stealing drinking water was fraught with the utmost danger; though he was carrying his own camelskin waterbag he had to refill it from time to time. The water was stored in wooden barrels and it took him a while to dip the cup into an open barrel and fill his drinking pouch. All the while, his eyes darted around anxiously and he'd only managed to half fill it before moving away softly.

But thirteen year old Amu had a mission, a mission for which he was ready to give his life.

His father had gone missing when he had voyaged, on a trading vessel, to the faraway land of Meluhha, the name given by Amu's people to Bharat. He had left more than three years ago and after all this time, Amu's family had finally tracked down a sailor who had last seen him in Meluhha, at a port town in its western coast called Lothal. This was exactly what Amu's father had told his family of the journey he was going to undertake. Now that he had a lead to follow, Amu was determined to find him. Or, at the very least, to discover what had become of him.

Amu was brought back to the present with sudden harshness. The sailor towered over him, and to Amu, never had a man, looked more menacing.

His heart thundered like a drum, and his mouth went dry. How was he to explain things to this man, he thought in despair. He knew he would be dropped off at the closest port; or, he thought dramatically, he would get thrown overboard. The ships carried people who could work hard, not passengers like him, who just depleted the ship's supply.

'Sir, Sir,' he stammered and then stopped, trying to appear fearless and bold.

The sailor, who was actually not just a sailor but also the captain of the ship, looked closely at the young boy, for his tough exterior concealed a kindly heart.

'What is it?' he asked, more gently. 'Tell me, for I can see you are weary and hungry, and I won't harm you if you tell me the truth.

Amu told his story haltingly.

'My father went to Lothal, in the land of Meluhha, three years ago, and has never been heard of since. I have two young sisters and two brothers. My mother is heartbroken, waiting all this while for him. She says he has not died; she says she knows it for sure... so I am going to search for him.'

The weatherbeaten captain looked at this young boy, who was watching him with a mixture of fear, dread, and defiance in his eyes.

For two long minutes the captain said nothing. Then he said 'Ok, I'll let you stay on board, but you have to do any job I give you. I will take you to Lothal, in the bay of Khambat, in Meluhha, and you can stay there and search for your father.'

Amu couldn't believe his ears. His expression changed at once. 'Sir, I'll do any thing, I mean anything at all, if you let me stay. No work will be too hard or too tiresome for me. Only, just let me stay,' he said, thankfully and eagerly, overwhelmed by the kindness underlying the man's gruff voice.

Amu was sturdy and stood tall, and was both sharp and emotional at the same time. He had brown eyes, which could either sparkle with mischief or darken with quick anger, depending on his mood. He was from the fertile land between the river Euphrates and the Tigris, in Mesopotamia. Theirs was a hierarchical, well-defined society, with priests and kings at the top, and Amu had led a comfortable life, learning the business of the family. He was part of a joint family and his father and uncles were all traders. He had often accompanied his father around the city when he was young. Now he went with his uncles to collect various goods. He was useful to them, helping them by gathering information about different craftsmen—who had better skills, who had more in terms of quantity, and who would supply them regularly. He had also quickly learnt to bargain and to buy and sell. The tragedy of his missing father had matured him beyond his age.

As the eldest of the siblings, he had assumed responsibility for his family, although his uncles and aunts, along with his mother, were the ones who ran the household. A man was always the head of the house and his word was law, and because his father wasn't present with them, his eldest uncle was now the head of the family.

But Amu's mind always turned back to his father, his father who had loved travelling; sailing the clear green-brown river that had taken him away from his family. It was second nature for him. Amongst his brothers, he was the one who undertook journeys. Voyages like these were fraught with danger, and it took a daring person like him to make them. Years ago, before he set off for Lothal, Amu's father, Enlil-zi-shagal, had gone to the far off land where the famous river Amu Darya, also called Oxus, flowed. It was the longest navigable river known. Enlil was amazed with what he saw. There were desert sands there, and rivers frequently changed course.

Precious lapis lazuli stones were found in the ravines of the Kokcha and Amu Rivers, and were traded in far off lands, where there was a great demand for them; Amu's father had brought back a pouch of lapis lazuli and everyone admired them. Amu was named after this life-giving river and always wore an amulet with a big blue lapis lazuli stone, for safe-keeping and good luck.

'You are Amu Darya, my life-water, my Amu,' he remembered his father saying to him. He quickly swallowed a lump in his throat. He remembered how he had left his home.

Amidst many tearful scenes, and after giving his word that he would take care of himself, Amu had set out on his mission, promising his mother that if his father were alive, he would find him and return home with him. She had sent him off with dried meats and fruits, and breads to sustain him on his voyage. He had tried so very hard to get on a boat, but no one would take him to Meluhha. And soon, most of the food given by his mother had finished.

Finally, he had been forced to become a stowaway. In the docks, he had heard talk of the large, wooden ship being fitted out for its trip to Meluhha. Unseen by the sailors, he had slipped in, hiding himself in the depths of the ship where the goods for trade had been stored. In the lonely darkness, he often thought wistfully of the fun and good times he'd had at home.

But now that he had been given permission to stay aboard, his mood changed; a great burden had been lifted from his shoulders. Now his journey felt more like an adventure. He helped where he could and became a favourite with the crew. He wasn't scared anymore, and played pranks and joked around. Of course, he got into trouble and was often scolded, but now that his secret was in the open, he was full of high spirits. The crew was from his own land, from the cities of Ur, Umma, and Lagash and Nippur and Kish.

He sang all the songs of his land, of old and far off times, and ancient events; he could sing beautifully. He even knew the epic 'Song of Gilgamesh'. His father had sung it, and so had his uncles.

The sailors, who had picked up the language of Meluhha on their trips, decided it would help Amu to become familiar with it, so they started teaching him. The captain decided he would only talk to Amu in this strange tongue!

' "Paani", water, Amu, now repeat it ten times.' He repeated the smooth word, rolling it around in his mouth. He knew how to say 'father'; 'pita or appa','amma', and 'ma', for mother and 'samudra' for sea.

The crew all chimed in, and Amu learnt many key words and polite gestures required in Meluhha. The sailors sympathized with the brave boy and hoped that he would find his father.

Time passed slowly on the ship; it seemed like months to Amu, but in reality, only two weeks had gone by! Amu had stopped feeling excited and was tired of the swaying motion of the boat. Up, down, up up up, down down, sway, lurch, toss and glide... he felt he now only knew the movements of the boat. There had been a few squalls at sea, when he felt he was pitched and tossed, but they had quickly blown over. Their crew had been very lucky, for they had had fair weather almost throughout, hitting only two severe storms, which had driven them off course. On those two occasions, Amu couldn't believe that the calm sea could become so violent and turn into a menacing gigantic water body, intent on swallowing them. Fortunately, they had a good, seasoned captain who saw them safely through it all.

Finally they sighted land. They arrived in the trading port of Sutkagen-dor, which lay between Mesopotamia and Meluhha in western Sindh, near the land of Persia. It was relatively calm here. Monsoon winds did not bring stormy weather with its dangerous currents and whipping, whistling winds, so trade carried on throughout the year.

'Ahoy there! We come in peace. Are you ready for us?' shouted the captain to the sailors and tradesmen gathered at the port. 'Yes! Come in peace, friends, we are awaiting your cargo,' called one sailor, waiting at the mooring site. Mesopotamia's land was rich and fertile, due to the flooding of the rivers there. Crops grew there plentifully, like sesame, wheat, barley, flax, and these were brought for trade to ports like this, along with other goods.

There was a flurry of activity on the wharf, for there were other boats as well, and Amu was left bewildered by all the action. Soon, their boat berthed, and they were ashore; sailors, traders, and groups of little children looking at the boat and them with curiosity. They had time to travel around, as their boat needed minor repairs.

After days and days of dried food, the crew thought longingly of fresh coconut water, lush, juicy fruits, newly baked bread and sweet honey. Human beings! Foreign people! Firm land under foot at long last! How they revelled in unrationed fresh water! On the ship, they had always been extremely careful, and not a drop was ever wasted.

The sailors walked around the small settlements, and were especially interested in the fishing village of Sotka-koh. Further east, the fortified settlement of Prahag held their attention, for it seemed an unimportant place to have such well guarded stone gateways. The local people explained; groups of marauding robbers had attacked the small villages, and this is why gateways had been built to protect the village and town folk.

As always, they traded and bartered some of their cargo for fresh food like dates and other fruits. Next, they collected a fresh cargo of different articles, which would be popular in Meluhha, to barter for the things they required when they returned back to Mesopotamia.

After a wait of a week, they finally set course again, for repairs had taken longer than expected. The boat was loaded with small supplies of turquoise and lapis lazuli, from the rivers Kokcha and Amu Darya, which Amu's father had brought back. The people of Meluhha loved these rare, glowing blue stones. They were worn as head beads and armbands. Interspersed with flat, round, gold beads, they became beautiful necklaces; some were fashioned into bangles and amulets, and some made into beautiful objects which decorated the homes of the rich and powerful. Amu saw the precious stones being put in pouches and remembered his father wistfully.

Then they were off again. The waters were tranquil and peaceful, with only a slight wind stirring them. Sunrise and sunset were times that Amu looked forward to, times when he stood still. He prayed to the gods of his land, to the gods of the sky, the wind and the water, to help him find his father. The silver of the breaking dawn, the crimson of the sunset, the sheer beauty around, made him hopeful. He would succeed, with help from the gods!

Slowly, they neared land. They spotted dark masses, which Amu was told were cliffs and islands; then the shoreline came into view. Tall silhouettes of coconut trees could be glimpsed, and their green fruit floated in the sea water.

Drifting now, they entered a gulf; Amu was told it was a gulf, as there was water on either side of the two arms of land that surrounded it. They were in the Gulf of Khambat, and yes, at last they were in Meluhha!

When the tide was high, the ship sailed into the estuary of the river Pavitra and docked at the famous landing stage at Lothal. As a port town, Lothal was well-known throughout the entire seafaring world. It was held up in the maritime world as an example of nautical engineering; a dock had been built there so ships could enter and stay moored at a docking yard. Built with tremendous engineering skill, it had a long, deep, rectangular tank with gates, which could be locked during high tide, so the sea water collected there. As the level of sea water in the narrow Gulf of Khambat was naturally high—higher by ten feet than in the Gulf of Kutch—the boats floated high enough to come in and dock there. Goods from near and far could thus be unloaded and distributed. At low tide, the silt brought by the river was cleared, channelled, and used in the nearby fields. All of this made the Lothal port a widely admired marvel.

The captain introduced Amu, who he had grown very fond of by now, to a few people he knew would take care of him. And after a round of goodbyes and formal leavetakings, loaded with a bundle of goods and a small pouch of precious stones to barter for food, Amu was on his own.

Amu looked around in wonderment, taking it all in. He stood tall, as always, but inside he felt very small and very much alone. Here was the place his father had voyaged to, the place he'd last been seen. Amu's magnificent quest, brave and perilous, had begun.

Little did he know just how dangerous it would be, or how brave he would need to be. He was going to face frightening enemies, know great terror, and feel much joy and sadness, before he met his family again. But first, he would make wonderful new friends.

Wild boar! A hair-raising rescue

About two months later, in the very same far off Meluhha, where Amu had journeyed to, a drama was unfolding: one that was to have far reaching consequences.

In the village of Anantpur, which had come up along the banks of the river in northern Kutch, young Kartik, who lived there, was busy with the usual chores his father had given him. His black hair blew in the breeze, and his dark brown eyes—so brown that they looked black really—were dreamy. His thin frame made him look younger than his almost thirteen years. But despite his skinny look, the hearty outdoor life—helping in the fields, playing in the sun, and swimming in the river—had made him wiry and strong.

He had been carrying bricks to the brick kiln, when he realized that he had left a few behind, and was returning to the far side of the fields to fetch them. He looked forward to meeting his friends once he was done with the last task and sped along briskly, his robe flapping against his brown skin.

After the morning's work was done, and as the older folk rested, the Anantpur children ran wild and played all kinds of games. He grinned as he thought of yesterday's game of hide and seek (which he thought too childish, but had humoured the younger ones by playing). How he'd frightened his sister Kaveri and his friend Namami by creeping up on them and giving a good imitation of a tiger roar!

Earlier this morning, on his way to the kiln, he'd had to shoo off the younger children, among them naughty Indu and Pervin and little Seema. Good natured Kartik could generally be trusted to be patient, so the little ones often trailed in his wake. They were constantly following him around and getting in his way, especially mischievous little Devathithi, who insisted on tagging along everywhere, and was constantly in some kind of trouble!

Kartik continued walking along the path when he noticed, from the corner of his eye, an unusual movement from the wooded copse to the right of him. He was walking slowly, as he was carrying two hard bricks in his hand. Ahead of him was little Devatithi, standing, completely absorbed in the bright blue bird sitting on top of a branch.

Kartik looked again, and froze on the spot... and then acted swiftly. He had seen a crazed-looking wild boar come into view, and Deva was right in its path. There was no time to call,time only for action. He had to head off the boar. He raised his arm and took aim, and using all the strength he could muster, threw the brick at the boar's head. Maddened, the boar tried to look around...

Meanwhile, Kartik had rushed and pushed the child away, intent only on drawing the boar away from him. Kartik then heaved Deva onto a branch, climbing after him, helping him. This took just a few seconds, and he was waiting for the roaring beast to be at his feet, ready to gore him, when he realized the enraged sound seemed to have stopped.

He turned from his perch, and found to his great astonishment, that the boar was slowly falling down, a surprised expression on his face.

Kartik had knocked him out cold, or rather; the brick had struck its mark as though it was an arrow shot with unerring aim. The brick had been the best weapon ever!

People from his village were there in a trice.'What has happened? Oh, this is unbelievable!' exclaimed one, looked at the still, unmoving boar, which was lying, dead to the world, on the ground.

Deva had started wailing, finally realizing what danger he had been in. He was plucked off the branch and was handed over to his father to be pacified. In the meanwhile, one of the village folk used his bow and arrow to finish off the ferocious animal. The boar couldn't harm anyone now.

What a hero Kartik became; more so, as he was known by all as a dreamer, and often had to be pulled up sharply when he would wander off, as would be obvious, to another world. His father was beaming with pride and joy. To think that Kartik, his gentle Kartik, had it in him to act so swiftly and bravely! Kartik told himself that it was just luck: normally his aim wasn't this good.

'Kartik, how brave you were! How on earth did you think so fast!' shouted Tatha, patting him vigorously on his back. 'Venkatanna, you must be so proud of your son! What aim! What reflex action!' exclaimed Chotubaba to Kartik's father.

'Yes, you have trained him well, for all his dreamy ways!' added Akku dada.

Venkat, or Appa as Kartik and the other children called his father, looked at everyone and smiled in relief. Everyone realized how brave Kartik had been, how swift and unmindful of the danger to himself, when he had saved Deva's life

Though his knees were shaking at the thought of what he had just missed, Kartik laughed the most, tickled to think that it was *he* and *his* aim that had knocked out the boar.

The village had a certain way of doing things, and the elders unanimously decided at a little conference they held, as was the tradition, to reward Kartik's bravery.

'And let's include Xerxes. He has put in such a tremendous amount of time and energy with this harvest—why, he's worked as hard as a man, though he's only thirteen years old!' exclaimed the chief of the village.

The next day Kartik went charging up to his best friend at high speed, yelling, 'Guess what! Xerxes, Xerxes! Great news! I've just heard! Just a few minutes ago! Just listen!' His face was flushed because he had run so fast.

Xerxes and he had grown up together, doing many things together, including landing in trouble, a number of times! Strong, fearless Xerxes was agile and tall and did most things carelessly, without thinking of the consequences. He had been both thrilled and excited at his friend's bravery.

The two were very loyal to each other, though they loved playing practical jokes on one another. Xerxes was the talker and Kartik, the quieter one, but just as ready for mischief. He could never say 'no' to a dare.

Xerxes was absorbed in drawing a map on a broad leaf, and Kartik only managed to get his attention when he drew close to him. 'You are coming with us... last night the elders decided. We are going to the Surya Mela, along with my father and the others. Akkudada, Nihalda, Chotubaba, Rajukaka, Amrobhai, and I don't know who else is going, but hey, *we* are, this year!' he announced with a shy, wide grin.

Xerxes gripped his arm hard. 'Has my father agreed?' he demanded, looking anxious. The Surya Mela was such a special event.

'Yes, and the girls are coming too. My mother says they deserve to, she says they are sensible and and have been so helpful this last year, when Mithilama was so ill, they must have this treat!'

'And all because you saved little Deva. What a wonderful reward!' exclaimed Xerxes, his face one big wide grin.

'I can tell you I was terrified when I was up in that neem tree… thankfully it had two low branches!' said Kartik with honesty.

In his excitement Xerxes began to stutter. He always stuttered when he was overexcited, though he was trying hard to be calmer. He could talk endlessly, and when he started on his favourite topics, everyone began to make a show of closing their ears, or slipped off, saying they had important things to do!

Both boys were singing with high spirits when the girls, Namamidevi and Kaveri, joined them. Kaveri was Kartik's sister and Namami was their friend. Kaveri was ten years old, the youngest of the four, while Namamidevi was twelve and a half, named after the spirit of the Narmada river, and often called Nomi, or Nami, for short.

The four were together all the time, and even the village people recognized the special bond they shared. They had rollicking times, playing pranks on one another, fighting and squabbling, but always sticking together against anyone who dared to criticize or bully any of the rest of the team, as they were called in the village.

Namami often chuckled when she remembered the time she had managed to lock Xerxes up. 'Tell me where you have hidden my little clay bullock-cart, and only then will I open this door!' she had blackmailed him. 'You'll have to, otherwise your father will find you, and you will get into trouble. Remember, you have to bring back the cows from the fields!'

'But wait, I won't let your precious dog Raja go to your house tonight,' Xerxes had retaliated, knowing how much Namami adored Raja. Dogs were their best friends and gave warnings of any wild animals lurking around, sometimes looking for fowl to steal and eat. Namami had laughed even more at this empty threat; Raja was intensely loyal to her and one whistle from her was all he needed to go to her, like a streak of loveable lightning!

She'd laughed, teasing Xerxes, knowing she'd won this round!

Of course their fighting was forgotten by the evening. At night, the whole settlement would sit in the dark, with a few fires lit to ward off wild animals. Music was an essential part of their lives and they had a number of instruments: an over-turned pot, the ghatam, a harp-like stringed instrument, bansuris made from reeds. Those who did not sing along just sat back, absorbed in the lovely music. Kartik and his friends would look at the stars, listen to what the learned astronomers had told the people in the cities, gaze at planets, and hear about how calculations were made. Sometimes they'd listen to tales of valour and adventure; of lands far away, beyond the mountains, of lands many seas away. And each one's secret dream was to experience such adventures.

Which was why all thoughts turned to the mela, now that they had been given the chance to go. Kaveri wanted to see the beadwork shops and the shank-shell artisans at work. She wanted to see how the beautiful necklaces were made. 'I'm bringing back amulets,' she declared.

Namami tossed her head and said, 'I'm going to the big warehouse granary with the sixty four rooms, and I shall watch all the merchants bargaining and bartering. My father has given me enough things for me to barter and bring back whatever I like.'

'Like what?' Xerxes asked her. 'All I want to see is the ships. What do you want with those goods?'

'I'm going to get a small set of bronze tools... a chisel, a hammer, and a rotating saw,' Kartik joined in. With a faraway look in his eyes, he announced, 'I'm going to see how the soft soapstone seals are made, then baked, or fired.'

And so, they dreamed on, only it wasn't to be a dream much longer; the mela was soon to become all too real!

Harappan times, 2500 BC: The journey begins

Barter? Seals? Amulets? Where and who were these children? And what was their story?

Namami, Kaveri, Kartik, and Xerxes lived in the years before Jesus Christ was born, in the year 2500 BCE, in Anantpur, which was in Meluhha, Bharat—the land Amu had travelled to.

The four children may have grown up together, but their ancestors came from different tribes and places.

Xerxes's great grandfather had come from beyond Avagaanaa, from the craggy, mountain regions of the north-west, where his father had come to trade the famed lapis lazuli of the rivers Kokcha and Amu Darya. Then he had come to Meluhha and settled in Anantpur. Xerxes' grandfather had given him four beads to put in his necklace, as a talisman. His parents farmed the land, tilled the soil, and of course, joined in the bartering and other trading that went on, like everyone else.

Kaveri and Kartik's parents had come from Kutch in western Bharat. Gifted artisans, they made the usual clay pots and urns, required by the villagers, besides some lovely and unusual shaped clay containers, which had never before been made in Anantpur. They had travelled to Anantpur and settled down in the same village. Before them, their own parents had made a sea voyage from the south. They were from a nomadic tribe, but had left the south, along with family, to try the mid-western lands.

Namami's parents were doctors, or vaids. They woke up early every morning, when it seemed like it was still night—all dark and misty, the birds sleeping. Then, with straw and cloth bags hung about them, they set off to collect flowers, leaves, and buds, still drenched with dew, to be made into medicine, which would cure illnesses. They covered hills, valleys, streams, and caves to find rare plants and Namami often tagged along, learning to recognize various medicinal herbs and flowers, some of which would be dried and powdered later.

The four children had rarely ventured outside Anantpur. Now, for the first time, they were going to leave their village and take a long road trip, by bullock-cart, to the land of ships and boats, and fishing villages.

The Surya Mela was held once every five years. People came from near and far for this magnificent event. It was held in honour of the sun spirit, at a time when there was a particular alignment of planets, at the confluence of the rivers Aravalli and Pavitra. All the spirits—air, sky, water, earth, and fire—were invoked, by priests, as well as all gathered there, on the last day of the mela. It was considered very auspicious to be present for this special configuration of planets. Everyone present was believed to be endowed with special strength and powers by the sun; the sun symbolized life, energy, purity, and power. Apart from its religious significance, the mela was also a place for trade, with stalls which sold cloth, jewellery, toys, including clever moving monkey-toys, various implements, bronze tools, and a whole lot of other items. Soon, the children's preparations began in earnest, and the following days were filled with great activity. 'Kartik, have you taken the sesame seeds?' 'Xerxes, carry those sacks there, one by one... and you, Namami, go help your mother pack all those different herbs and powders... and be careful, mind you!' This was all they heard all day.

They helped the grown-ups, who were going with them, put together a huge collection of goods to be traded at the fair. It would just about fit in the six bullock-carts that were going to take them there. They were to carry all the grain that Kaveri and Kartik's father could harvest, breads, fruit, dried foods, shawls, and other odds and ends which they could possibly barter. What a motley lot of bundles there were! Also, they would carry various articles, given to them by the village, to be bartered in order to bring back things they needed, but didn't grow or make.

This was common practice. Some people came from Amri, known for its pottery, near Mohenjo-daro. Some came from far off Roparrani on the banks of the Sutlej, famous for its wonderful timber, and some from the icy Himalayan mountain reaches. Many of the people who lived near the rivers Jhelum, Saraswati, Sindhu, Beas, Ravi, and Sutlej would also try to go, though this was mainly a pilgrimage for them. Some would use river transportation and some would travel in carts, starting months in advance. The Surya Mela was truly a holy journey for them.

Finally, after five more days, the preparations were complete. On their last night at home, the four huddled together around the fire, wondering how they were going to sleep that night. Suddenly the adult voices trailed into silence, as two strangers appeared by the fire. They spoke with great politeness.

'We were sailing down the river and wondered if we could ask of your hospitality this evening, it is too dark and dangerous to continue sailing,' the older man said to the village chieftain. 'Certainly. You are most welcome. Our home is your home. We will see to all your needs this night,' was the response. In Anantpur, and all of Meluhha, offering hospitality to strangers was an important custom.

Kaveri looked on with concentration, and the others also watched in utter silence.

The men made themselves comfortable; they were traders. 'Have you heard the news of a great robbery in Mohenjo-daro, some weeks ago?' they asked. The entire village gasped in shock and the air was filled with the murmuring of hushed voices. Xerxes, Kartik, Namami, and Kaveri looked at each other, eyes round and gleaming with excitement. A robbery! Robberies never happened! This was unheard of! And in Mohenjo-daro, the most glittering city of the land, on the banks of the river Indus. It was the golden city of riches and plenty, which everyone was longing to see!

The elder man explained, 'It was from the temple. The chief priest-king's headband has been stolen. Also, five golden statues, five bronze statues, jewels, and the carved incense holder, studded with precious stones. It is a real mystery. The guard was assaulted, and then tied up, and the celebrated dancing girl statue has also vanished overnight! Everyone is talking about it, because the headband was made of the most precious stones and gold, and the dancing girl was very valuable.'

'They have no idea who was behind this?' Appa asked the travellers. 'No, and what's worse, the priest-king had in his safekeeping a precious object from a fellow chieftain of a neighbouring town. This too has been stolen and his honour lost.'

The conversation carried on late into the night; no one could stop talking or asking questions about the robery. None could believe this impossible news. Robberies were extremely uncommon in this region.

Namami's mother came bustling up and said firmly in the midst of all the excited chattering, 'Children, you have a long journey ahead of you. Come on, its time to go to sleep.' 'But we can't go to bed now. We are too excited... just a little later,' pleaded Xerxes. But the elders wouldn't hear their pleas and with much grumbling, the four friends were sent off to sleep.

The big day finally dawned. The journey was to commence in no time, and the last minute organizing soon took over everyone's thoughts.

Namami looked around her house as she packed her powders. She saw the family's two deep red pottery urns, on it black borders featuring animals, peepul leaves, and some intricate designs. They were exquisite pieces and had been given to her parents when they had helped save the life of a young boy, the son of a tribal chieftan, who had thus expressed his gratitude with the gift. The urns were a matter of great pride to the family. Namami hoped to bring home more such beautiful things from the mela, including tales of all the different sights and sounds.

Kaveri was busy at her own house. 'You have to stay with Nami, and listen to her,' her mother was telling her. 'She'll look after you well. And of course your Appa is with you.'

Kaveri's mother put one of the beautiful hair clasps she made, of shell and bronze, on her daughter's little head. She also made many kinds of necklaces, and was an artist. She could draw beautifully, sitting for hours at a stretch. Her long garments wound round her, and every line she drew seemed to come alive. She'd look at a squirrel, half shut her eyes, and the next moment, she'd make a beautiful drawing, full of life and movement.

Next, she put Kaveri's favourite clay bangles on her hands; Kaveri loved the sound they made every time she moved her hands. The clay bangles were coloured with a red dye. Once as a surprise for her, Kaveri's father had brought them home for her; she had been so delighted! She often tried to dress like her mother or the other ladies; sometimes with long lengths of cloth wound round her, and other times, such as in winter, in skirts with tight-fitting blouses. She longed to colour her lips with red tree bark and put rouge on her cheeks, like some ladies did on special occasions, but had been forbidden to do so by her mother, because she was too young.

The team got all kinds of instructions from their parents. 'Be careful. When you take shelter at night in the way beside villages, show your gratitude.' 'Show respect to your elders! Show that you are true children of Anantpur!'

As they stood with Appa and the other grown-ups, ready to go, their younger brothers and sisters hung around them, clinging to their hands, reluctant to let them go.

'We'll bring you shell bangles,' Kaveri promised the little girls.

'I'll get you the most colourful clay toys,' announced Xerxes.

Kartik's small friends looked at him. 'Yes, you troublesome little folk, I am going to bring you something special, but it's a secret, so you have to wait,' he said teasingly.

Kaveri ran back all of a sudden and gave her mother a last hug, her lower lip trembling slightly. Her mother gave her a hug and kissed her, saying softly, 'Have a good time, my little one.'

Her father, Appa, came and pulled her plaits. He laughed, 'Come now, or we'll have to leave you behind!'

Namami hugged her dog, Raja, whispering to him to take care of everyone. She gave her parents a hug and almost choked Raja with her tight last hug.

After these emotional farewells, the children got on their cart with Appa and they were off! Trailing behind them were the other adults—Akkudada, Nihalda, Amrobhai, Chotubaba, and Rajukaka—in their carts carrying the heavier goods. As the six carts, pulled by strong oxen, rolled out of the village, their passengers waved goodbye to everyone, promising to bring back wonderful wares and presents.

The route was long, and carefully planned. They had to cross wooded areas often, but these they crossed safely, as they were not as thickly wooded and large as the jungles. They took the long route to avoid the jungles, which could be dangerous. Even then, they would have to be on the look out, for although they used the mud roads, wild and dangerous animals could creep up on them unexpectedly.

The first day set the pattern of the next five days. They left in the cool of early morning, and continued with short breaks, daily. The further away they went from Anantpur, the more the vegetation seemed to change. Great trees stretched overhead, providing much needed shade. Sometimes when there was a tree laden with familiar fruit, which Appa was sure they could eat, the group obligingly stopped.

Between bites of plump, round ber, Kaveri announced at their first stop, 'This is the best ber I have ever eaten. Fruit tastes so much better here!'

The carts trundled on and when the sun was directly overhead, they stopped to rest the bullocks and refresh themselves near a stream, in a little wood.

'You know, my mother remembered the soap nuts, gave them to me in a packet and told me to wash the clothes with them, as well as myself!' twinkled Namami, for she knew the boys had deliberately left theirs behind.

'Err, umm,' said the boys, and ran away from the reach of Namami and her soap nuts!

Returning from the stream, they enjoyed the cool canopy of the trees around them : the forest trees, with their lovely flame of orange-red flowers bursting off the ends of branches; the boab trees, with their huge five foot girths and odd shapes; cork trees, which were plentiful in Anantpur as well. Thank god for trees!

They started again after the heat of the afternoon had subsided and came to the village they were to stay at, that first night. 'Greetings to you,' said the villagers. The group from Anantpur was enjoying the hospitality of the village of Belapur.

'And to you too,' they replied, as they got down from the carts and made their way to the two rooms kept for them. Tired from their travels, the children were soon asleep, each cosily wrapped in a shawl for warmth.

They travelled on steadily for the next few days. Once they came to a pond and saw the water birds, which had migrated from the snow lands. What a variety there was! Painted storks, a slash of bright pink against a patch of black on their creamy bodies; white cranes; pelicans; egrets; all flying over the pond, looking for fish, and then alighting on to a nest atop the trees surrounding the pond. The children were fascinated.

They had already become more aware of all the animals around them, even the bullocks which were bearing them towards Lothal. The creatures were sturdy and strong, used for ploughing fields, but they had to be looked after with love and care. There was a routine of caretaking of the animals to be followed each time they broke journey, and it was Namami, of course, who loved all animals, who followed it patiently. She always talked to them and stroked and patted them when they were resting, or after they had finished eating. Appa watched her, amused, while the boys always vanished to explore the surroundings wherever the crowd stopped for rest.

After three more days though, the novelty of travel wore thin. The children were tired of the jerky, jumpy movement of the bullock-cart, and squabbles broke out. Xerxes managed to get hold of Namami's multicoloured rocks and threw them out, saying they added weight to the cart! This made Namami wild, of course. Luckily, Akkudada stopped everyone in time and waited till she found them. Next, Kartik pulled Kaveri's plaits and she pinched him back, hard. The slightest thing led to an argument, which had to be sorted out by one of the others, and Appa had to speak sternly to them.

Yet, despite all disruptions, their cart had moved far ahead of everyone else by the fifth day and they were almost at Lothal, as Appa kept telling them, when suddenly the children heard an alarming noise—c-r-a-ck! Something had given way: their bumpy little cart had lost a wheel!

Everyone got out and gathered around the cart. For a good half an hour, everyone tried their best to fix the wheel. Eventually Appa gave up.

'You children go ahead by foot, the others will catch up with me and then I'll come,' he decided. 'Meet me at the east gate this evening, if I don't catch up with you by then, near the small granary, not the one at the dock yard. Will you remember? Kartik? Xerxes? The small granary has some rooms nearby, so go there and wait.'

Everyone perked up. This was a new thing, to be on their own... an adventure! Xerxes had a gleam in his eyes when he looked at Kartik, plotting and planning already, and the girls fussed about their things, excitedly.

Appa calmed them down, warning them that they would have to be responsible. 'Take your small bags and bundles with you, some food, and the shawls, it's always good to have your own things with you.'

Xerxes, Kartik, Namami, and Kaveri all picked up their own small bags, which contained what each considered the most important thing in the world that they absolutely couldn't do without. Appa would have been surprised if he knew what had gone in there!

They were ready to leave, but looked apprehensive, to Appa's knowing eyes. But he knew there was little danger, as they were very close to the town.

He reassured them, saying, 'We have already crossed the jungles and are now in cultivated land, so you will meet many people going to the mela. You will be safe, that is the most important thing. It's just a few hours away. Xerxes and Kartik, you are in charge. And if you need help with anything, find Altair.' Altairbhai was a young man from a neighbouring hamlet, and he was also to be at the Surya Mela.

He hugged Kaveri and Namami and gave Kaveri's plaits an affectionate pull as always; it was their very own special signal! He patted the boys on the back, a small line of worry on his broad forehead. 'Do be careful, and stay alert,' he told them seriously.

Then he cleared his face and smiled. 'Well, enjoy the long walk you lazy lot, after all the sitting, you will be happy to walk!'

'Appa, we take your leave,' said the four children, and after final instructions from Kartik's father as to where they would meet, they began to walk on, chatting gaily.

Kaveri, in great spirits now, kept pointing out all the new things she saw. It was a constant refrain of 'Look at the little green tailor birds! Look at these nests, they are weaver birds... See the little porch they have made with grass? Aren't they clever? Look at that pond, see the lotus flowers... Will we see a tiger?'

She carried on like this till Xerxes asked impatiently, 'Kaveri, what's so new? We have weaver birds too. In fact, we have beautiful, tiny yellow and blue sun birds, with curved beaks... Calm down! What's all the fuss about?'

'Because we are on our own, with no grown ups,' she grinned. 'Ok I'll stop now,' she giggled, giving a huge mock sigh, and everyone laughed loud, all in high humour. Nothing could keep them down now!

Joker... and an elephant ride!

Xerxes, Kaveri, Namami, and Kartik set off at a brisk pace, enjoying the feeling of their newly acquired independence. After some time, feeling hungry, they decided to take a break. They sat down under a beautiful flowering flame of the forest tree and ate their lunch, feeling happy with the world.

'Hey, I wonder what people in Lothal are saying about the great robbery,' said Kartik, out of the blue. The others all pricked up their ears at this. The excitement of the journey for the past few days had pushed the dramatic news to the back of their mind. 'What kind of people could have committed this wicked act?' wondered Kaveri. 'Can you imagine if we were to ever meet the thieves? Would you be able to charge at them Kartik like you did at the wild boar?' teased Namami. Xerxes was about to offer his own theory when they were interrupted by someone most unexpected.

They heard a small whine, and Namami perked up. She looked around, and a small puppy appeared from the foliage around them. He was tiny, and with his black fur, white patch over one eye and one ear flopping over the other, he looked like a comic little fellow!

Namami called to him at once, and he came hesitantly, but wagging his tail. She stroked him and spoke to him softly. The puppy licked her hand, then put his small paws on her waist and licked her face gently.

Questioningly, he put his head to one side. He seemed to be asking, 'May I stay with you?'

Namami squealed as she felt his soft tongue licking her cheek. She patted him and gave him something to eat. From then on, he was like her shadow! The rest of the team called him Nami's dog.

'Look, he's smiling,' exclaimed Kaveri, surprised.

Namami scratched the dog behind his ear and he gazed adoringly at her. Then he lay down on his back, his stomach exposed, as if saying, 'I trust you totally.' She scratched him again and he gave a small, satisfied bark. Namami whistled (she could whistle very well) and the little fellow cocked up his ears at once, and putting his head to one side, looked all the world as though he understood that this whistle was especially for him! He gave a short, happy bark and licked Namami's hand again, wagging his tail all the while.

'We're keeping him,' said Namami at once. Of course, this was a popular move.

'What should we call him?' the children wondered. 'He's so affectionate... Moti, no, Chotu,' they argued, going back and forth till Xerxes decided, 'He's so funny, let's call him Joker!' Everyone laughed at this.

'That's clever,' said Namami approvingly. The two had finally made up after their squabble over her rock collection.

Promptly, the little puppy was adopted by the group, and dubbed Joker.

They decided to move on, little knowing that more good luck awaited them—the team of five were to snag an elephant ride!

It happened in the most unexpected way. After lunch, they walked ahead slowly, talking loudly all the while. They were so loud, in fact, that they cleared the woods, on either side of them, of creatures who had dared to venture near the path they were following. They came across a little clearing, and in it was an elephant grazing calmly. The creature was eating a huge amount of green leaves and grains, and Joker barked curiously at this sight.

The elephant's keeper, the mahout, lay lazily in the shade of a nearby tree. He was a square, stocky man, with long black hair that was tied back, and a flowing beard. Hearing the children chatter as they advanced, he sat up and smiled at them.

He looked young and and his dark face had a cheerful look to it. Most of all, Kartik noticed, that his eyes were friendly. He looked like someone they could trust.

The children gathered around the mahout at his invitation, and he began to chat with them.

'What are your names, children?' he asked, jumping up and studying the group.

Xerxes introduced each of them to the mahout, even little Joker who was dancing around excitedly. The children all gave him the formal greeting they were taught, mindful of the instructions Appa had given them.

'My name is Robida,' grinned the mahout. 'Now, were you just talking about Lothal? I overheard you. Are you going there? We are also going near Lothal, to the ivory workshops there. I can give you a ride. But you will have to sit on these bales of cotton.'

Xerxes was the first to answer, as always. 'Yes, please sir, we'd love it. We are going on our own, though my friend's father is following behind. Thank you so much.'

Namami asked hesitantly, 'Er... please may we take our puppy with us? He won't leave me.'

'Yes, if you can keep him in your lap,' was Robida's reply.

Namami was thrilled and promised to do so. Kartik did two rapid somersaults in succession. The first elephant ride of their lives!

They all stood for a minute and looked at the elephant with curiosity—and a little awe. She was SO big. Tentatively, Kaveri asked if they could pet the elephant.

'Go ahead, my beauty loves people. She is very gentle, hahash-ho! Those gentle pats will only tickle her. Do this.'

'Thump! Thump! Thump!' went Robida, giving gentle slaps and thumps to the elephant, on her side.

The girls followed suit, becoming increasingly bolder, and approached the trunk of the elephant. Her name was Champakali. She was happy to hear their laughter and stroked them lightly with her trunk. How they squealed with laughter when it tickled them!

They examined her tough skin, her wiry hair, her cream ivory tusks, her huge, strong legs and feet. At last they clambered up, agile Xerxes doing so easily and Kartik followed suit. Champakali had lowered her great bulk down, so this was not too difficult. But then she started to get up, much to Kaveri's and Namami's disappointment.

'Never mind, I'll tell her to pick you up and put you there herself,' Robida assured them, seeing their crestfallen faces.

'Champakali… churr churr churr kook kook koookkii kookkii!' he told Champakali, in a commanding tone. (This is what it sounded like to the girls!) Stroking her trunk, he was getting her to pick them up, as he had promised.

'Now don't be scared,' Robida told them, and Namami and Kaveri resolved not to let the boys see that they were indeed scared.

Suddenly Namami felt the rough trunk wind itself around her, and just like that she was lifted up! In one minute, she was sitting on the elephant, just like the boys, on the wooden seat that was strapped on there. Just like on the swing she had at home, hanging off the two branches of a tree, there was a swaying sensation to everything. Kaveri soon followed, laughing, absolutely delighted. They much preferred the way they had climbed the elephant, the girls told Robida.

Robida followed, expertly holding little Joker, and patting Champakali gently, he whispered his special word of thanks to her. Again, these were noises the children couldn't understand, but Xerxes tried to imitate them. What fun it would be to be a mahout!

And so began their first ever elephant ride. Sitting amongst bales of cloth and sacks of grain, all four spoke at once, telling the mahout about their village. Or, as Namami liked to call it, everything that had happened to Xerxes since he was born. After all, there was nothing like a captive audience!

Atop Champakali

'How different everything looks from here! And how far ahead we can see!' exclaimed Kaveri.

Everyone talked and laughed from their lofty perch, enjoying the swaying, side-to-side motion of the elephant's walk. Robida smiled as he listened to their excited chatter. 'I've got a small son and daughter, and they just love Champakali!'

He told them about his home nearby and his children, and they in turn told him all they had heard recently, about the outside world, from people who had been passing their village, travelling down the river.

'Has anyone here heard about the great robbery at Mohenjo-daro?' asked Xerxes.

'What great robbery?' said Robida.

'Don't you know? The chief priest-king's headband has been stolen,' began Kartik, going through the whole shocking tale.

'No, none of us here have heard of the robbery, you are the first visitors today from the north,' replied Robida, aghast at the news.

Kaveri told him of the shock in the town

of Mohenjo-daro when this major theft had been discovered.

The little girl described things in such detail that the mahout was impressed.

Although she was the youngest and looked small and delicate, with her long, dark hair and coal black eyes, Kaveri was very strong and determined by nature and had a quick and ready understanding of things.

The others all interrupted her at this point and added more details of the crime to make Robida see how serious this robbery was to the people; their whole security system had been penetrated, beaten, their honour tarnished.

After a bit, they began to notice and remark on their surroundings; all the aspects of it, which were different from their own village.

'So many temple pagoda trees, it is a whole grove of them, we have so few in Anantpur! Look at the waxy cream flowers! And look at the long flat pods of that tree!' exclaimed Namami. 'I wonder what use they have. How come we don't have those?'

'Because it's a Gulmohar tree, and they don't grow in our village,' explained Kartik, who sometimes managed to come up with little bits of knowledge which the others didn't have. He had been upstream with his father a few times and seen the different vegetation there. In the process, he even had some idea of the names of a few trees.

Eventually, of course, the conversation returned to their favourite topic: all the things they would do when they got to Lothal. The lure of the unknown was as strong and forceful as a magnet.

Of course, all four children were curious, all for different reasons.

'I'm waiting to see how well I can barter,' confided Kaveri, with her engaging smile. 'It will be the first time I will do it all by myself, you see. What am I looking for? Carnelian beads!' She remembered her mother's pretty etched beads of deep glowing red. She wanted toys as well, especially the animals with movable heads which went up and down on a string; and the carts with wheels. She would imagine that she could go to faraway lands in them.

'I'll see the workshops where they use the bronze tools to make the seals,' singleminded Kartik said, with great anticipation, looking at the two small terracotta seals, threaded with a small precious stone, given to him by his father to ward off evil. His village mainly made pots and urns, using the potter's wheel.

'I'll learn to carve figures like fish, snakes, bisons, unicorns, and gharials, rhinoceroses, or even a Zebu bull,' he added. 'I'm going to be a master craftsman.' He twisted his hair impatiently, wishing it were longer; it was the adult men who wore their hair long and braided, and often shaved their upper lips.

Namami, who had now thrown off her cotton shawl and was crooning to the huge elephant, had listened avidly to the stories of Lothal which had been told over the last few days and stored them away in her sharp mind. She thought about all the exciting possibilities ahead.

They would actually see the upper town where the noblemen lived. 'I wonder what we'll see? We'll see a big bath—does every big town have one? At the dock, we'll see the trading when the big ships come in.'

'Tides! Moon phases!' thought Xerxes, his light eyes alight with interest. How much he would learn! Maybe he would see the learned men who calculated the tides and moon phases and then worked at the hydraulic systems of the ships. Maritime trade absorbed his interest completely. 'We are going to the dockyard at Lothal and will watch a boat unloading. After the tide comes in, there is a lot to see,' he volunteered to Robida. The people of Jayanagar, the village they had stayed in the previous night, had told them about it.

Xerxes was determined to make the long voyage to far off Egypt, and other places, from where these ships came. Ever since he had been a young boy, stories of the sea, storms, the different customs of various people of these far off lands had interested him. He loved the river, and his greatest wish was to be a sailor.

He made a sudden confession to the others. 'I'm going to exchange my animal skin cover, my leather robe, for a boat ride in the sea,' he announced.

Everyone was shocked into silence. Animal skin covers were especially expensive, as it was usually people from freezing mountain villages who hunted the thick-furred animals, and made them into garments. One had to barter huge amounts of grain, or part with precious stones or gold to get one. It became almost common property for the village, and Xerxes's home had one belonging to his great great grandfather.

'Xerxes, you will get into trouble. Does anyone at home know you have brought your animal skin coat with you?' asked Kaveri, eyes wide, clutching his arm in anxiety. Clan punishments were sometimes harsh and though Xerxes's parents were easygoing, this could call for a clan meeting and tough punishment.

'And,' thought Kartik to himself, 'no one's parents would allow one to trade something so essential to us in cold weather.'

Xerxes said with a hint of desperation in his voice, 'You know I may not have the chance to go to the sea again. My family is just not interested in moving anywhere, but my ancestors were! See how they came here... I must be like my great great grandfather, who came from beyond the far off land of the river Kokcha. He came through the famous Khyber pass, wandered, traded, then crossed the Sulai pass through the mountains and ravines, then the Bolan pass... But *my* parents will stay here for the next hundred years! Look at the other tribes, the one that came from Mohenjo-daro, who brought us news of the robbery, remember those two men? And the others who had come earlier, they come and go every year.'

Namami reasoned with him. 'But they are gypsies, it's in their blood... they only come to the plains to graze their goats and sheep during winter, as it is too cold in the mountains. They live such primitive lives, no proper houses, they move all the time… and this time the whole tribe didn't come, only two people came, and they were traders; the ones who told us about the robbery.'

'But how will I learn about seafaring ways, about tides and the workings of the ships unless I go out in a sea boat one day?' asked Xerxes, his eyes flashing passionately. 'You know how I love the river, so can't you imagine how I'll love the sea? It's supposed to be vast, endless and so still. H-o-w, h-o-w, h-o-w… H-o-www I wish… ' He had started to stammer again, so stopped.

'And what about all the fruit you love: jackfruits and mangoes? Who will plant more trees? And gather the fruit? And grow barley and wild-rice?' the others fought back. Robida gently and skilfully changed the topic, and after a few minutes, their attention turned to Joker, who was still sitting on Namami's lap.

Namami pulled at her long loose gown; it wasn't the most comfortable outfit for an elephant ride, she decided ruefully! But it was useful for keeping little

Joker comfortable in her lap, so she just grumbled, not really meaning it. The elephant walked with long, ponderous steps, and everyone swayed and jerked and then shrieked with laughter.

The lands all along the Indus river had forests, as there was abundant rainfall. The centre of dense jungles were teeming with animals... tigers, rhinoceros, and other animals. There were herds of elephants, and some had been domesticated, as had the cattle and ass. Wild ass too could be seen near the drier parts of the land.

Just as the children were ready for a halt, they saw ahead of them a young couple, standing next to a cart. The animal was standing next to the man and woman, but the wheel shaft of the cart was broken.

'Oh, stop! Stop!' called the young man. 'We need to go to the coast urgently. My wife is sick and we have relatives who have the medicines to cure her. But now our cart is broken, we can't go forward.'

Robida yelled, 'Ok, we will give you a lift. What about the animal, though?'

'Oh, he knows his way back. Our village is very close-by, if you know the short cut, and Doddu has gone that way a hundred times.'

The young man pulled out a large sack and a few bundles, and led his wife forward. She had covered her face and head with her shawl, so they only saw a small smile on her fair face. She was obviously the shy sort, so they didn't talk to her. Looking at the couple, Joker set up a shrill bark.

It was Kaveri, surprisingly, who managed to shush him into silence, and she moved him from Namami's lap onto her own, for the time being.

The young man kept checking to see if his things were safe. He seemed more worried about his sack and various bundles than anything else, least of all his wife, thought Namami, who was used to observing the sick people her parents treated, and their loved ones.

Getting Champakali to sit down so the couple could climb on took a while, as she had decided to be difficult! After the third attempt, and Robida's gentle urging, she lowered herself to the ground and the couple got on.

'Have you heard about the great robbery?' asked Xerxes after some time had passed by, trying to make conversation.

'What robbery... we don't know anything, do we, wife?' replied their new co-passenger.

Xerxes proceeded to tell them about it. Namami, tired of hearing about the great theft, began again on that more exciting topic of what she would barter at Lothal.

'See my whistle?' she asked Xerxes 'I'm going to trade it for a squirrel or a metal pin with an animal head.'

'No, give it to me... I love it' exclaimed Xerxes, who particularly wanted this whistle, which was shaped like a bird and made of terracotta.

Namami refused, and her bright eyes filled with laughter. She winked at Kartik and said solemnly,

'Only when I get a ride in a flat bottomed fishing boat going to sea, will I give this to you. You have to find one and arrange it for me. You are so crazy about boats, and the sea, now do something and show me that it's not only talk, but action too.'

Lothal at last!

An hour or so later, weary—an elephant ride wasn't as comfortable as they'd imagined—the children were ready to walk again. They were leaving Champakali alone again; the couple they'd picked up along the way had gotten off surprisingly soon after they'd gotten on, taking all their bundles and chattels with them. Xerxes asked Robida to let them off a few miles away from Lothal so they could stretch their legs before getting to their destination.

After bidding both the elephant and mahout goodbye, with many grateful thanks, as well as an open invitation to come to their village any time for a visit, they walked on, talking animatedly among themselves. Joker was most eager, prancing around them and waiting to play his favourite game—fetching sticks.

Kaveri kept interrupting with her usual chatter, while Xerxes wore a thoughtful look on his face.

'Hey, what are you thinking about?' inquired Kartik, noticing how engrossed his friend was.

'I was thinking of that man… there was something different about him. His village must be much farther away than ours, for he doesn't know our customs. He would never have offered to give barley in exchange for the ride from Robida, if he was from nearby.'

'Yes, we never do that,' Kartik replied. 'And he didn't say a word to any of us... just sat silently.'

'Queer ways these other people have!' said Namami, putting an end to the conversation. After all, they would never see the strange couple again!

Soon they were near Lothal. There were more people around and more fields under cultivation; there were also fruit orchards of mango and chikoo trees. This was the village Morvinagar, closest to Lothal. A small stream meandered near them, a small tributary of the Pavitra river.

'Just look at the difference in the speed of the water!' Kartik pointed out. In the far distance, the stream came swiftly over a rocky shelf and there was a small, cascading waterfall, glinting and sparkling in the sunlight. The water came down with a great rush, its bubbling white foam frothing at the base of the rocky ledge. It then wound around some big boulders and small rocks, seeming to change its mind, and became a peaceful little stream, meandering close to them.

'Let's wash in the stream,' suggested Kartik, voicing everyone's thoughts, and they all plunged in at once. Having lived all their lives by the riverside, they were expert swimmers. All villages were by the riverbanks, just built higher up, so floods didn't damage their houses.

Joker lapped up the water as he frolicked, then sat down, an idiotic grin on his face, tail wagging nineteen to the dozen, as though to say 'Yeah! That drink of water was great!'

A quick swipe afterwards with Amma's precious ivory comb, and they were all neat and tidy. Now for a taste of city life! Now to actually be in a town! And experience everything there!

'We are supposed to meet Appa near the granary, this evening. Let's quickly walk through the Morvinagar fields, and get to Lothal as soon as we can. We can explore the place till we have to meet Appa. Only, no one is to go alone anywhere, and if anyone wanders, please use the whistle each one of you has,' ordered Xerxes, as leader of the group.

They walked and walked, taking in the sights and sounds, of small brick rooms, two or three together. They seemed to be workshops of some kind. They watched, wide-eyed, as they passed a monkey, doing tricks. He was on the shoulder of a young boy. The boy saw them and grinned. He started to juggle some fruit he had with him. First he used only two, then three, and finally, with great skill, he was juggling four. Successfully! The children gazed in admiration, Xerxes wishing enviously he could do the same. Then they burst out laughing, for the monkey started imitating the boy and juggling fruit as well!

Moving on, they passed a large maidan. One side had small hillocks, and they got a glimse of water as well. Now they were almost in Lothal. In the maidan, many people had made little camps all around, and from the look of things, people from as far away north as Akhnoor, which was on the river Chenab, had come. Also were people with their wares from as far as Harappa and Roparrani in the north, and Meghrgarh in the northwest of the Indus river, Mohenjo-daro, and Bansiwali. Closer, were the Kathiawadi people, from Dwarka, Ranginapur in western Kathiawad, famous for its chert-stone blades, and closeby Kuntasini, known for its carnelian beads. From areas near Madhapur, near the hills of the west, came other tribes. This was going to be a great mela! There were groups of families under a clump of neem trees; some were strolling around, some had already made little stalls, ready to barter their wares.

The four children spent their time wandering around, exclaiming and looking with wide-eyed wonder at all the new and unknown things they were encountering.

Namami was immediately struck by the medicine corner. They were all kinds of herbal remedies for things like upset stomach, cuts and wounds, colds and coughs. But here was a difference: there were medicines Namami had never heard of! She knew of tulsi, aloe vera, neem, and other common plants, roots, and barks of trees near their village, but here were unknown dried fruit and berries, along with various roots.

'Lets get her away before she finds out what those dried, awful looking powders are,' suggested Kaveri in alarm. She had had endless experiences of Namami and her medicinal remedies. 'Remember once when Amma was away and I had that dreadful cough and bad throat, and she wanted me to have that terrible milk and haldi, and I ran and hid?' she recalled with a grin.

The others chuckled. Namami often imagined herself as a doctor.

'You will be here all night, Nami,' scolded Xerxes, but his eyes crinkled into a smile. He knew exactly how Namami felt... he was just as crazy about the sea and boats, wasn't he?

It was now getting later than they'd thought it was; the sun was lower and long shadows were cast on the ground. They decided to hurry to the granary. A sturdy young boy walked past them as they hurried along and gave them a bright smile and waved. He pointed to the dog and made a gesture signifying, 'He's nice.'

Something about him struck Namami and she said to the others, 'He looks different, but I like the look of him.' They waved back, not knowing that they would soon meet him again.

Greeting strangers was nothing new for them now; they had wished so many strangers, and spoken to so many new people today. Just the fact that everyone was here for the same reasons made them feel like they all belonged together.

They reached the walled town of Lothal proper, at last. 'What a pity it is getting dark, we are really late... we won't be able to see anything of the dock,' said Xerxes, regretfully.

They walked to the high ground near the small granary. 'Look at the wall! How thick it is! Well, I guess it keeps out flood waters,' explained Xerxes.

'If we don't see your father, we'll just find a sheltered spot and wrap ourselves in the shawls and sleep,' announced Xerxes.'

'But only after eating! I am starving now!' announced Kaveri, with a grin.

They entered the east gate, but there was no sign of Kartik's father, or the other people from the village. 'What's happened to Appa?' asked Kaveri, sounding worried. 'Oh, he'll come, don't worry,' replied Namami. They went a little further away, to a long, low brick building, from which they could hear the sounds of merchants.

'Oh, look, there's Altairbhai. We'll ask him where to sleep,' said Namami, spotting a familiar face. They approached and greeted the tall young man Appa had told them to find, and told him what had happened.

'I think the best thing for you to do is stay here, they may have had some other delay, but there are six of them, so don't worry,' Altairbhai told them.

'Hey, you!' he yelled to one of his friends in the marketplace.

A man came over, and when he was told what had happened, he led them all into the low building from where they had heard the merchants. They went through two passages, into a room, and Altairbhai's friend told them to rest there for the night.

'Let's just go see the market, and maybe we can eat there as well,' said Kartik, sniffing the lovely aromas of food cooking. They went to the market, which was close-by.

Fish! Namami's mouth watered. She had been hungry, and was even more so after smelling the delicious scents which wafted on the air.

It was like a mini circus. Women had built small fires with clay griddles on top, and there were also fires built under flat stones. Fish wrapped in leaves was getting roasted on the burning hot stones. Fish was frying on one fire. Small mud ovens cooked roasted meats, and there were various new eatables, which the children had never eaten or even seen. They were just longing to taste some of these exotic treats. Clay pots with curries simmering in them, the smell of sharp new spices, barley soups... the list was endless. People had come from far and near and brought what they grew or had stored, or had got from elsewhere.

Kaveri and Namami decided they would have the fish, which had first caught their fancy. Kaveri looked at the dish wistfully. Her mother made the best fish curry ever, pounding spices, adding green chillies and haldi to them, and ground sesame seeds; the frying fish was bound to remind her of home.

Namami touched the little girl's hand gently as they chose their supper. She had often gone with her father to pick medicinal plants, and had stayed away from home for days at a time, but she had a feeling that Kaveri was a little homesick, as she had never left her mother before.

For the moment, they had to figure out what the women would take in exchange for this meal. Most of the things they had hoped to barter were in the bullock-cart, as Appa had been sure they would meet by now. So, they had carried only a few essentials and favourites with them when they had left Appa. Xerxes put his hand in his bundle, slung like a bag on his shoulder, and took out some things they could barter. Kaveri approached the lady. She thought for a bit and then pulled out the long, new scarf her mother had proudly given her. Giving the woman the traditional greeting, she said, 'Please may I have that,' pointing to the fish. 'I'll give this to you. I need enough for four of us,' she said, pointing to the scarf.

Looking at dark-haired, coal-eyed Kaveri, with her dazzling white smile, the lady laughed and said, 'I have plenty of food and I don't barter with children... take this and more.' So saying, she wrapped up the tangy smelling fish in green leaves and gave it to Kaveri.

'Thank you so much. Where are you from?' Kaveri added added hesitantly. She didn't know if it was polite to ask. Everyone at home was particular about good manners. So of course she'd kept her palms open outwards, hands stretched out, as she had been taught to do, and head bent down. The former was to symbolize that there were no hidden arms, no knives or stones; and the head was always bent to show respect.

The lady nodded and patted her head, accepting the show of respect, and blessing her said, 'I'm from Dholavira. A mela like this is so auspicious, and a whole group of us have come here. The spirit of the sun is truly the most powerful at this time and at this place, where these two special rivers meet.'

Kaveri and Namami sat and watched her skilfully pat dough into rounds and put them on the griddle. She turned them over deftly. She poured butter from a jar, and oh, the tempting fragrance just tickled their noses till they felt they had to eat at once.

Kaveri's mother had always said, 'You children are so lucky. When I was young, my grandmother made very few varieties of food. Now different foods and spices come from great distances, and I can cook so many more dishes for you. We always had the same things day in and day out.'

Funnily, Xerxes was the only one reluctant to try new foods. He enjoyed only the foods he knew.

'What a waste, Xerxes,' Namami teased him, 'you will go to the lands over the seas, and you will only want pea curry and sesame bread and lentil dal. What's the use of going to new places if you don't experiment and taste their foods? Now if I went, I would try all different dishes and enjoy them as well!'

'You're welcome to do that, Nami,' said Xerxes with a grin, 'but I like what we eat in Anantpur!'

The lady gave them some chutneys—seasoned mixtures of strange leaves and nuts pounded together in combinations they had never tasted before. With it, they ate the new bread they were trying, called thalipeeth. They loved this new tangy, sour taste of the chutneys, together with the thalipeeths. Joker had found his own food and came back looking very pleased with himself, licking his lips. But he had a guilty air about him as well. Namami guessed the truth; 'The naughty fellow, he's stolen some meat, or begged for some and got it.'

'Well, he's lucky he wasn't given a sound thrashing and sent off,' said Xerxes, sounding amused. You just couldn't help loving and petting Joker, even when he'd been a little thief!

The foursome looked around the marketplace a little more, then settled in a corner to play the games all Meluhhan children played. They had a lovely collection of small conches and played a game of conch-thief, or shankh-chor, each grabbing a shell and then seeing who could collect the most, by means of an elaborate set of rules.

The noisy game continued till Kaveri yawned, a couple of rounds in. This set everyone off, and they decided to go to sleep. So back they trooped to the long hall.

They took with them the leaves of the mosquito bush, which kept mosquitoes at bay with its strong smell. They scattered these leaves all along the straw mats Altairbhai had given them. This was a neccessity, as mosquitoes led to a shivering fever and illness, which was often fatal.

The four found a corner, snuggled under their shawls, and went off to sleep. Joker, of course, stuck to Namami's side and after going round and round by her side (as though he was in a field of grass and had to shape the ground beneath him into a bed!), happily went off to sleep.

Everything was so right with their little world. Nothing could have prepared them for what was to happen the next day.

Lothal dockyard

Early next morning, Namami was woken by Joker's frantic licking. She'd been dreaming she was swimming in a river. 'Oh, it's your tongue,' she exclaimed sleepily, as she automatically patted him, and hugged him to her.

Joker kept pulling at her till she realized he wanted to go out. Yawning, she woke up the others, and they all collected their things and went out. The dew was still fresh on the leaves and buds as they stepped out. A few drops seemed to be suspended, glittering with rainbow colours. The children wondered when Kartik's and Kaveri's father would come. Akkudada's or Chotubaba's carts might have suffered some damage, they thought, as they had been lagging so far behind. Also, no one travelled in the dark.

'We'll see them today, not to worry. So let's see the dockyard first,' said Xerxes, eagerly.

They went to bathe in the river. A quick dip and they were out. They started the chanting that they had been taught to do every morning, in melodious voices; a homage to the elements:

In the beginning there was creation
The sun, earth, water, and air
All created only to give us generously
Everything we could ever need
We live because they give liberally
We bow down saying bless us
Help us always
We give honour, love, respect, and gratitude
For all the bounties received
Continue to guide us
Continue to provide for us
Oh Sun, Earth, Water, and Air
Our humble thanks
Our humble salutations
Be with us, guide us for ever

Namami tried to dry Kaveri's hair with a cloth, and then just combed out her long, black tresses. The wind would do the job of actually drying it. Her brown face shone brightly, and her dark hair really looked like the river Kaveri!

Sitting around the gnarled roots of a banyan tree, they ate a hearty breakfast and looked around. All kinds of people were there, praying or meditating, giving thanks to the life-giving river water spirit. It was like ten worlds rolled into one for the children, who had never in their lives seen so many people at one time, all engrossed in such deep spiritual activity.

The confluence of the rivers was some miles away, and it was where the religious chants would be heard on the auspicious day, which was four days from now. Till then the trading and bartering would carry on.

'Come on, let's go to the dockyard. Now,' said Xerxes firmly. He thought he had been patient enough!

After asking for directions, they were on their way. Some minutes later, they were at the dockyard. People were busy. It was high tide and a boat had just docked.

'Look at the height of the water and waves, its high tide so its nearly eight to ten feet more than anywhere else... like Dwarka,' they overheard.

'This boat has come from Persia, beyond Sindh, and that one is from Dilmun, west of here and Falaikka island in the Persian Gulf, it has pearls from Basra... they are going to have a pearl market special.' Talk buzzed around them. They listened, eager, and thrilled, to imagine they were about to witness a real trading mart.

This was so different from the humdrum of their daily life, where they helped in the house and the fields during the day, and gathered at night by the fire. They were happy enough there, of course, but as Namami said, 'Nothing exciting ever happens to us... we work, we play, we study, we sing songs, and listen to stories of long ago the sutradaar tells us... but nothing more exciting than an animal killing happens. Travellers from places as far as

Mohenjo-daro and Harappa bring us news… but nothing happens to US!'

As the children looked at the dockyard, and heard the hum of activity around them, they felt that they had the chance to witness something exciting at last. It felt as though a ballad had come alive in front of them. Bigger boats than they had ever seen on the rivers were tied to a couple of mooring posts.

There was a landing stage and on higher ground there was another platform for all the goods to be kept after unloading. This was part of the upper town, where the noblemen and rich merchants lived; in short, the rich and the powerful. There were five men, checking to see if the seals were unbroken on the goods that had come in. They wore long robes and had chains around their necks. Their long hair was wound around their heads, and their beards and moustaches were very grand and imposing.

'We have to meet a sailor who knows all about oceans, some one who is the rajan of the sea, the most experienced!' said Xerxes, almost reverentially. He had done his homework.

The children kept exploring. There was a granary very close to the docks, built at a height, and this was used as a storeroom, sales room, and special market. Grain was stored here and the ruling class was in charge of its management and security. Right round this ran a wall cutting off the upper town from the lower town, where the potters, fishermen, artisans, and craftsmen lived and had their workshops with furnaces and ovens installed.

'I can't hear myself talk... there's such a hum around!' grinned Kartik, turning back to the dock. 'And they say we kids make a noise!'

There was shouting, talking, loud yells, as many packages and wooden boxes were unloaded, and yet everyone knew exactly what to do and what was happening!

'See the new boat,' said Kaveri, pointing to a brand new boat, to which finishing touches were being applied.

'It's made from teak wood... very good for boats,' Xerxes told her, smiling at how much little Kaveri was enjoying the sight of one of his beloved boats. Kaveri grinned back. She was determined to make the most of this trip, and was keeping her eyes wide open!

Xerxes was absolutely quiet, his green eyes shining with excitement and sending out sparks of fire. He was mesmerized by the seafaring atmosphere of the place. Grouped on one side were the merchants, their merchandise tied and sealed, all ready to be sent to the far off lands of Basra and Egypt and Mespotamia. The others let him be as they knew it was a dream come true for him.

Suddenly Kaveri burst out singing. This was a gift she had; she could make up songs within a few minutes, some funny, some sad, but always very interesting! She spun around and around, her arms held aloft, and softly the words floated…

The sea, the sea, open and free,
bringing treasures from far and near.
All of you must come and hear,
stories of the sea, the waves, and the wind.
Pearls from Dilmun, cotton from Egypt,
when will I go there and share the wonders…
Skim the waves in a boat, feel the salt spray in my hair…
Xerxes loves the sea so green
I want to swim in this water as in a dream…

Twirling around she danced and danced, and amused onlookers clapped their hands to see a young girl so filled with the joy of living.

Meanwhile, Xerxes had found a sailor who was quite taken up by this enthusiastic lad and ready to explain many things which puzzled Xerxes. Maritime engineering, as the sailor told him, was based on a profound knowledge of sciences; of observation, common sense, and calculations. He explained how the locks worked, so water would stay high and the ships could stay afloat. 'See, the tides push the water higher here through the narrow mouth of the gulf of Khambat, the waves are higher than any coast nearby.'

The others found Xerxes with the sailor and soon gathered round with their own questions. What a lot they would have to tell everyone at home! Namami had two young brothers and a little sister, and Xerxes had two brothers and two sisters; they, and the rest of the village, were waiting for them to return with stories of the Surya Mela. They would describe the colour of the dock water: a brown green-blue colour, as it was sea water that had come in with the tide. The various people, the different clothes, hairstyles, the buzz in the air… oh, so much to tell!

'Our life is so simple at home. Our games of hop scotch, langdi, chase the wild animal, our chess matches, our games with rudraksha beads,' remarked Kartik.

'Yes, the games at which we always beat you boys,' laughed Namami, throwing a pebble at him.

The great house of grain and goods and trade

After an hour, they prepared to go to the east gate to check if Kartik's father had finally arrived, exploring on the way. 'Let's go see the Great Hall,' suggested Kartik, and they went to the high-raised store and trade house. This was used for trading, for sending parcels, labelled and tied, to far off lands across the seas.

The long building there was made of the same baked bricks which were to be found everywhere in Lothal, but this one had a long passage and what seemed like many big rooms, to either side of it. In reality, they were not very large, and each housed a whirlwind of activity.

What confusion seemed to reign! Chert-weights, beautifully polished and exact in weight-measures, were on the straw mats, along with bead-stones, which were to be weighed; bales were being sealed; people moved sacks around from one end of the room to other. Merchants shouted, 'Throw that seal away, it's cracked!' There was the din of traders bargaining, and owners checking that their stone seals bore the particular symbol, which identified them as owners. These would be stamped on clay or steatite soapstone tablets, and had a knob, also called a boss, with a hole, which was used as a tag. They would then be attached to bales of goods, using string that went through the hole.

Kartik was in heaven. The others moved ahead, but Kartik lingered near the seals, riveted by the drawings and carving he saw on them. There were seals with drawings of bisons and a unicorn, which was held to be very lucky. Xerxes' sister had a talisman with a carved unicorn on it, back home. The unicorn was a common symbol, used very often. Next, he saw a rectangular tablet with the pictograph,common at that time, of a deer with antlers, looking over his head, along with writing symbols. There was also a soapstone seal bearing the stars, sun, and moon; often seen, as many calculations were carried out using the position of the sun, stars, and planets. This Xerxes had told him. He picked up the bits of broken tablet which lay around examining them curiously.

Near him stood two men, examining a beautiful, three-sided, moulded tablet. Kartik saw it and shyly asked them if he could see it.

'Oh you want to look at it? It's worth looking at, let me tell you,' said one of the men. 'It's been carved by Kritimaan Kalakaar here, the best carver! See, we use soft soapstone steatite; it's easy to carve.' The quieter craftsman only nodded. Kartik eagerly took the tablet in his hands, and looked at it keenly.

Kritimaan Kalakaar explained his handiwork, and showed him the other seals. One side showed a flat-bottomed boat with two birds sitting on the deck, the second side had a snout-nosed gharial with a fish in its mouth, and the third side had eight symbols of the pictorial Indus script.

Kartik was amazed at the great detail that was used in the carving. 'Sir, how do you carve such thin lines to show details like eyes? It is so difficult! The seal is so small!' Respectfully thanking the master craftsman Kalakaar, he reverentially returned the seal.

'One day, my seals will be here,' he vowed. Kalakaar was so impressed with the interest shown by Kartik that he called one youngster and told him to show Kartik everything. So Kartik got the most amazing guided tour. He watched the bales covered with reed sacking, containing cloth and other articles, being tied by reed rope and sealed with the hot melted wax. These would be sent out in ships to far off lands, some would be sent inland.

In the meanwhile, Xerxes had found someone to talk to, who would tell him even more about the sea, while the girls were in another room, looking at lovely craft items which were carefully being packed. Jewellery, shank shell bangles, necklaces, and other items, all neatly sorted and coded.

One section just had stored goods, which had come from far off lands, for the seals were unbroken. These would be sent upriver by riverboats, or by land on ox-carts.

Kartik eventually rejoined the others, his flushed face shining with pleasure. They continued down the long passage to a room which had bales of cloth piled high against the wall; at the other end stood two men, obviously talking about business. As they walked in, a strange sight met the four children's eyes.

Amu's story

A young boy lay behind a bale of cloth by the wall, hiding. He was visible only to them it seemed; it was the same, sturdy boy they had waved to the previous evening in passing, when they'd first entered Lothal. Only now he looked a little worried.

'We meet again,' Namami said to herself, feeling an immediate empathy for the boy. Why was he hiding? It didn't look to her like he was playing a game.

The boy turned to them and his eyes widened in recognition. 'Sssshh... ' He put his fingers to his lips to tell them to keep quiet. Xerxes crossed over to him silently, and the boy pointed to two men who were talking softly across the room so intently that they hadn't noticed the children walking in. They looked familiar although Xerxes couldn't place them. 'Go out now, quickly. And avoid them,' he whispered to Xerxes, as the others watched, out of the corners of their eyes.

It was obvious the boy didn't want himself or them to be noticed; they quietly slipped out through the long passage to the big hall, where some packages were stacked. From here they reached the big door, which took them outside.

They went out, and Kartik said softly, puzzled, 'Xerxes, did you notice one of those men? The tall one… he's the one who took a ride with us. But he's changed his clothes and is wearing a short animal skin as though he has come from the icy mountains, and he's got clan amulets.'

Kaveri and Namami soon joined them, bringing a reproachful looking Joker with them. They'd untied him from the post where he had been tied before entering the granary. How he barked his disapproval at them!

'Why did that boy ask us to leave?' asked Namami. 'And what was that man doing here, I wonder?' mused Xerxes. While they were talking, the fugitive boy came up behind them softly, running lightly and pressing himself against the wall, so as not to be seen.

'I am Amu Darya,' he said. His accent was different, the others noted.

He bowed his head, as a sign of friendship, and put his palms forward, opened outwards, in a symbol of peace. Yes, here was Amu, the stowaway, who had come to Meluhha to look for his missing father! And now he was meeting Xerxes, Kartik, Kaveri and Namami, all of whom would prove to be an important part of his quest.

The four huddled around the boy curiously. They instinctively trusted him; he had a smiling, open face. He was not from their land, or at least they had never met anyone like him. But like them, he wore a short, knee length robe, with short sleeves. His eyes were light brown, set in a light coloured face, and he had curly, red-brown hair. On his arm was an amulet of blue stones, and his neck bore a black thread, with a glinting blue stone on it.

'Listen,' whispered the boy urgently, 'let's go somewhere quiet.'

They walked on and stopped at a tamarind tree nearby, where many people were passing by. This way they wouldn't be conspicuous in the crowd. There were oxen, and goats, grazing. A monkey swung by them swiftly, chattering and jibbering away as though he was laughing, and as Kaveri looked at him with a smile, he pulled her plait and darted off as quickly as he'd appeared.

'Oh Kaveri, you wanted to see a monkey dance and now you've had a special one all to yourself!' shouted Kartik with laughter, watching his sister look indignantly at the tail of the impudent monkey. Kaveri stuck out her tongue at him, and said with assumed dignity, 'what's there to laugh?'

Amu had started talking, but he too stopped and started laughing when he saw the monkey's tricks.

Hearing his free, unaffected laughter, the children decided that whatever Amu, with his bright, sunshine-filled face and ready smile, was going to tell them, they could believe. Instinctively, they felt he would speak the truth. How could you disbelieve someone who looked at you straight in the eye?

They introduced themselves to him, smiling, and sat down.

In broken Mehluhi phrases (how glad he was that the captain had taught him the basics, and he'd improved too in the last two months of travelling), Amu told them his story. 'I am from Mesopotamia. Those men were talking in the Sumerian tongue, which is mine as well. We speak that language at home. I overheard them talking in my language and saw inside the taller man's robe, a lapis lazuli amulet and necklace like mine, which is a clan sign. I am looking for someone from my land and I thought as they spoke my language, they might have a clue to give me. But when I began to approach them, I heard them talking about a stolen treasure and how it is to be sent to my country when the boat leaves after two days... I was so surprised because our country is very strict with thieves and criminals. We hardly have any crime at all. That's why I quickly hid myself. They also talked about four children and a dog. And a bundle, a mix up, which was the wrong one. I had seen a puppy with you last evening and I thought it might be you when you walked in. That's why I made you rush out.'

The four sat up in surprise. They hadn't checked their bundles last night; they were too tired.

'Thank Xerxes for tying Joker to that small post outside, before we entered the granary! And it's good you have him here now, Nami!' said Kartik, in relief, motioning for everyone to move somewhere more private, to check their bundles.

They wound in and out of small groups of people, and found a sheltered spot, near some red hibiscus bushes. Sitting on the rough grass, they quickly opened their bundles.

Amu now told them, in detail, about the conversation he had overheard.

'There was some talk about gold figures stolen from Mohenjo-daro, an elephant ride. I couldn't make out, but it seemed as though one of your bundles got mistaken for theirs, and they have a problem. They travelled with you.'

Xerxes exclaimed in a rush, 'You were right, Kartik, that man in the corner, he must have been the one on the elephant with us. That's why he looked so familiar! Only he looked different, earlier he wore our kind of robes, now he's wearing an animal skin, as though he's from the snow mountains... and the other man with him, may have been pretending to be his wife.'

'Yes, and we would not know as she was draped with a shawl and fully covered. No wonder they left in a hurry when we mentioned the stolen treasure,' added Namami, excitedly.

'And they, they are connected to the great robbery in Mohenjo-daro! I can't believe it! To think we were sitting next to them!' interjected Xerxes, giving Namami a clap on her back.

The other three looked thunderstruck. This really was an adventure.

'What robbery?' asked Amu. 'There has been a daring robbery in the grand temple of Mohen-jo-daro' said Xerxes. 'We have heard of nothing like it,' and with this he filled Amu in.

'Let's look at all our bundles,' decided Kartik. As they spread out their things, there was a shout from Kaveri. 'Hey, this isn't mine. There's a lady's skirt here, and a knife, and a man's pouch. Mine had my tops and my terracotta toys. Oh and my small doll and my tiny bird whistle and squirrel!'

'Look at that little package inside the skirt,' said Namami, going over to Kaveri and peering at the bundle she had somehow ended up with. 'It has a packet inside it. See, it's lumpy!'

The girls opened the cloth package, and found a roll of cloth in it, with figures, symbols, and pictures in red on it. Inside this was a dirty, waxy looking figure, quite heavy, but dull looking. There were bits of a clay tablet, too.

'I wonder what all this means,' said Xerxes, thinking aloud.

'I think we should give it to my father and be careful till then,' said Kartik in a worried tone. 'He'll know what to do.'

'Yes, we should really tell just your father, and not talk about it till then,' agreed Xerxes.

'Let's go to the east gate, to the market, those are the only two places he'll be. And if he's come he'll have waited for us,' decided Namami.

They walked off, chattering away. Each was secretly wondering what exactly would happen now that the strange bundle had been found. Asking Amu Darya all sorts of questions about where he came from, telling him about life in their village and of the various towns they had heard of in this vicinity, they found that talk of agriculture was common to all of them; of dry spells and irrigation, sweet water wells, floods and fertile silt, rain water harvesting.

But how long could one talk about this everyday stuff, wondered Xerxes, looking enviously at Amu, thinking of all the other exciting things one could discuss, like exploring distant lands.

'You travelled in a boat from Mesopotamia. You have seen the sea and experienced a sea voyage. How lucky!'

Amu replied, 'Yes, it's so wonderful when the ship is going high up and then right down. You feel the sea will swallow you and ugh uhugh... your tummy!' He clutched his stomach and made grunting noises; rolling his eyes and making silly faces. He was, generally, extremely funny, the others decided. How he made them all laugh!

He told Kartik about the wonderful artisans of his land; they made beautiful objects for burial rites. Gold figures, cups, plates, numerous articles studded with precious stone, to be taken to the afterworld with the person who had passed away. Immense importance was given to this. People spent their life earnings on these beautiful objects.

'And your shank shells are famous there as we don't have them. I heard you only get these shells in the shallow waters off Kathiawad and Kutch. They make conch shells in gold in Mesopotamia , copies of your conch shells here.'

The children realized how different things were in Amu's land from their own customs, which were so simple. They had no temples like those Amu described, called ziggurats. Theirs were low, wooden buildings, with a holy significance to them; not grand and imposing step towered structures, like those Amu described. Ziggurats had stairs and a temple on top, holding statues and ornaments and altars; priests lived here. The people believed that the gods lived in the heavens, but when they visited earth, they stayed in the ziggurats.

They also had special scribe schools, where children of rich families studied; in Anantpur, there were no scribe schools like in Mesopotamia, but they'd all been taught to read and write on barks and leaves; even little Kaveri knew their script, which ran from right to left. Amu, on the other hand, had never been sent to a scribe school. His land though really was the most fertile, as it was between two rivers, unlike the dry, arid land surrounding them; when the rivers flooded, the rich silt was deposited, and made the land fertile.

They were a prosperous people, reaping a rich harvest every time, and able to barter it easily.

'But we have no monkeys,' he laughed 'Oh that is one thing people in my country love: monkeys! I want to take one back with me when I return,' announced Amu.

The others screeched with laughter at this great ambition of Amu's—to take back a monkey. Imagine, a land with no monkeys!

Amu knew a short cut to the bazaar, so they arrived quickly. 'Oh, I can smell fish being fried!' exclaimed Kaveri.

'I can smell a spicy vegetable curry!' They got the whiff of roast meats and soon they were close enough to see griddles with various kinds of breads cooking. They could also see different kinds of sweets made with delicious fresh honey. They got the whiff of sweet sheera, made of rice and milk, which they loved; it was a great favourite. Anantpur mainly grew wheat. It was lunchtime and everyone was ready to eat. And they had a new friend to enjoy lunch with! They found a nice spot under some trees and took out what they thought would be enough to exchange for food. Between them all, they managed a fair amount.

Kaveri went to the same lady she had gone to, the day before; fish spread out tantalizingly in front of her. Mmmm, the lady cooked with lovely spices.

Namami went to get different kinds of sweets, and 'thalipeeth', of course, and the boys got wonderful fresh peas, green and sweet, and spinach curry.

Joker too managed a good meal; the market folk around them had given in to his pathetic 'I'm starving' look. He sat with a sad, patient look on his face, and promptly wolfed down everything given to him.

'Looks as though he's starved... He's just too clever, the rascal,' said Namami with an indulgent smile.

They had a feast, and drank plenty of water afterwards. Feeling sleepy, they all stretched out and lay down for a short nap. Joker sniffed around nearby, and then he too turned round and round on the rough grass and went to sleep.

'What are you doing so far away from home, Amu?' asked Kaveri sleepily, just as she was dropping off to sleep. 'Where are your parents? And who is the person you're looking for?' Kartik, Xerxes, and Namami looked at Amu with interest. His face, so relaxed a few minutes ago, had become dark and sombre.

He looked consideringly at them, then nodded his head as though he had made up his mind. He told his story.

Haltingly, he explained about his lost father and how he had come to Meluhha to find him. He told them he had arrived two months earlier, and had moved around from village to village, from sparse hamlets to bigger settlements. 'See, I even went to Namaksagar and Neelamabad, but no luck', he said with a catch in his voice. 'He looked sad and defeated. 'I travelled by ox-cart, on camel back, by river boats, I walked so much... I went with anyone who was willing to take me along. I wasn't willing to stop my search, then. But now... ' His voice trailed off.

He had tried his best to find out something about his father, by asking people and listening to conversations.

His tale was so gripping that Kaveri began to chew her plaits, as was her habit when she was engrossed.

'I tried so hard to find some lead as to where he could have gone, or how he vanished so completely. But I have had no luck... except that someone from Dholavira said something about a new member of his or her tribe. I heard this only yesterday. I have been to Ranginapur and Kuntasini, I have gone to Dwarka and Okha, I heard about Khadir byet, and so many other ports... ' He added, with a break in his voice, 'I am almost ready to give up. I have been bitterly disappointed so often.'

He stopped talking, and all four children looked at him with a mixture of sympathy, sadness, and concern.

Kartik struggled to keep himself from bursting out, 'Imagine not knowing where your father is!' He thought to himself, 'I would be so frantic and so unhappy.'

Amu looked so sad and alone that little Kaveri jumped up, linked her arm through his, and said—'Amu, no, no, don't give up. You were alone before, but now we will help you. Really we will.' Her tender heart was touched by the idea of Amu and his family waiting for a father who had never come back. Everyone nodded in agreement. They were sure, the four of them—wait, the six of them! With Amu and Joker included in the team, they could now solve the mystery of this disappearance, together.

After this they they dozed a little, except for Xerxes who lay awake, still wondering about the meaning of the cloth scroll. At last, he too yawned, and dozed off.

He woke up and opened his eyes with a start, a little later, worried. He woke up the others, saying very soberly and seriously, 'I think we should hide this in a safe place till we meet your father, Kartik.'

The five agreed, and Amu, who had been in Lothal far longer than them, told them he knew of a very safe place.

'It's deserted and I have taken shelter there many times,' he explained. 'I'll take you, it's the other end of the great granary, so it's much quicker to go from here.'

Kaveri had been looking on, wide-eyed, and promptly put the end of her plait in her mouth; her perpetual bad habit. Quick as a flash, Namami pulled it out, warning her, 'Kaveri, you are NOT to, your mother has told me to look after you!'

'And who bites her nails?' asked Kaveri cheekily.

'Stop arguing, you two!' muttered Kartik, looking worried.

They set off, walking fast, only little Kaveri skipping along.

Hiding the scroll

'I know all the short cuts, so we'll be there soon,' said Amu. They entered the upper town, where all the noblemen and officials lived, and passed several brick houses with flat roofs and courtyards. Sunlight made the baked brick glow, and trees cast dappled shadows on them. It all looked very calm and tranquil.

The children looked around with curiosity. 'The roads are much wider. And look,' Kartik said, 'no open drains, so it's just like our village, no foul smell of any kind, and it's so breezy.'

As it was afternoon, and the roads were quite deserted; everyone was taking a quiet nap, a respite from the heat of the day. The children were glad for they didn't want to be noticed as they went about their little mission.

They watched a lady walking by, dressed in brightly coloured robes, wearing flowers in her hair, and as she passed, they got a whiff of a fresh fragrance, which seemed to make the day just a little cooler. They had seen other well dressed ladies in town in the morning: wives of noblemen, with their fancy and elaborate head dresses and hairstyles, rouged lips and gold ornaments. How elegant they seemed, and how different they were from the simple women of their small village.

The Anantpur foursome noticed even more differences (Amu was used to all of this now). The roads here were broad, and smaller roads intersected at right angles. They had been built in a grid pattern.

'It's really a well planned town,' observed Xerxes, thoughtfully. Peering at the walls around each house, he pointed out, 'See the trees planted which give plenty of shade.'

Seeing public drinking wells, which were evidently there for travellers, they were further impressed. Amu told them that each house had its own brick-lined well, close to the door, a central courtyard, and even a separate bathing area; all the dirty water connected by pipes drained into the connected sewers!

'My land has open drains, ooh, you should smell the stink sometimes, when the wind is in the wrong direction! And roads curve any which way... there is no planning!' he told them.

The air was fresh. Some double storey houses looked big and gracious, and the children compared them to the homes in their village; single storey huts, large parts of them for storage. Rain trees had been planted all along the road and some were in blossom, so the pretty colours caught their eyes.

Amu urged them ahead, saying, 'The third cross road has a well, which has dried out. It is a nobleman's house, but no one lives there now….'

They reached the third cross, and saw a walled area with a house within. Amu quickly climbed up the wall like a cat! He was checking to see if anyone was passing by, but all was clear; the place was deserted.

Joker had vanished and Namami kept whistling for him. The others, in the meanwhile, got impatient and went ahead; Amu told them to climb any of these trees and jump into the garden from their overhanging branches. They were all very agile and fit, having spent so much time at home climbing trees while playing hide-and-seek, or in search of fruit. Namami was still looking for Joker, but jumped over at last, reluctantly.

There was a covered well in the corner of the open courtyard, and they ran to see it. Amu moved the cover off, and they peered in. When he had first come to Lothal, he'd explored the town really well. He had seen this house, and knew it was deserted, because the well had dried up.

'See, there are footholds and I can easily climb down. There are small gaps where bricks have been removed, so we can put that map or whatever that packet is, along with the dull looking object.'

Just then they heard a 'Woof! Woof! Yap, yap!' There was Joker, looking so proud, laughing at them and saying 'See, I've come!' Namami and the others were quite proud to see that Joker had found his way in.

They then took out the little packet and examined it properly. The little grey figure didn't look the least bit interesting, so no one bothered with it. The cloth with the symbols and pictures on it was certainly more intriguing. The bits of clay seemed to bear some kind of carving, but no one could make out what it was... part of a tree?

'Let's copy the scroll, then put this one away to hand over to my father,' said Kartik, very sensibly.

After a small search, they found a piece of broken brick and some old sacking material. Quickly and accurately, Kartik drew out the map, or whatever the strange drawing was. He was really a born artist, and could draw very well, so they soon had a replica of the original.

'And let's keep these bits of clay tablet,' suggested Xerxes. 'In fact, let's try to solve this riddle. Come on, everyone, this is a mystery. We never get a chance to do anything like this,' continued Xerxes, impetuously.

He added, 'Wh- wha - what fun if we children find the treasure or wh- wha- whatever it is... ' His eyes were shining; he had begun to stammer, the way he always did when he was excited.

Namami's eyes sparkled with delight. There was no end to what they would have to tell everyone in the village!

'Yes, let's,' agreed cautious Kartik, pretending to be calm. But even *his* cheeks were flushed with excitement. 'It really is intriguing, and we are in the middle of things,' he agreed finally, grinning.

'It should be fun,' he added in his innocence, little realizing what they were up against.

They were about to set out on an adventure bigger than they'd ever imagined! Everyone was exhilarated. It was a novelty to be alone, without grown-ups, and with a mystery all to themselves. Joking and making wild guesses about the map, and the meaning of its various symbols, they got quite carried away. Even Joker began to bark wildly!

When they became serious again; they looked more carefully at the scroll. The sun, three hills with a piece jutting out like a crocodile snout from the side, a moon and some stars; on one side, water. Two lines or waves, and a strange script.

'Some boats!' shouted Xerxes, thrilled, and everyone laughed.

'I think it is the cuneiform script,' said Amu. 'It certainly looks like it, it is wedge shaped.'

'Is that the script of your land?' questioned Kartik, ever the artist, studying the strange symbols, which were pleasing to the eye. Amu nodded. 'I wish I could read it, but as you know I was never sent to the scribe school.'

'Is it a river, sea or the dock? There are boats… and what is this cross in the middle? Are these stones or rocks? The hills look like the ones we saw on nearing Lothal.' They puzzled and puzzled over it all, then gave up for the time being. It was a real riddle, and they wouldn't be able to find the answer so easily, they knew.

'Let's hide it,' suggested Xerxes, reminding them of what they had come here for.

'That corner has a moon... how queer!' exclaimed Kaveri, still reluctant to put it away.

'Forget it' said Xerxes, shortly. All of a sudden he felt uneasy. The girls were young and till Kartik's father rejoined them, they were his responsibility.

'Yes,' said Kartik quickly. He was frowning, and there was a line of worry on his forehead. Although he was excited about solving the mystery, he had doubts now. Just a short while ago they had been so carefree, it had seemed perfectly alright to take up this new adventure. But he wondered if they should have told a grown up, and taken advice from someone who might know better.

'I think we should keep these bits of clay... they look like bits of a seal to me,' said Kartik, suddenly. 'I've just seen something that looks familiar. It may be something important, we don't know. In fact, we should figure out what it is. I'm going to try and remember all the carved seals I saw in the big granary today.'

He stowed the bits away, and they wrapped the scroll and the dull figure in straw and old sacking, making a neat parcel of it. Then, Amu Darya, who seemed to be an expert at climbing (he told them that being on a ship had made him as agile as a cat) went down into the well to hide their find. They decided they'd mark the spot with bits of shank shell that were lying around. Namami put the packet in some straw, so it looked old and commonplace, and no one would suspect it was important, if it was found.

Amu took the package and quickly climbed down the dank well. When he was about six feet down, he found a small niche and hid the small sacking in it, then put the shank shell in front of it, and last of all, little bits of brick. Now no one would be able to find it!

He climbed up quickly, and feeling for the same footholds, he was up in a matter of minutes, back in the bright sunshine.

Kartik had been unable to resist studying the seals again, as he waited. He spread them out quickly, while the others were watching Amu, and said, just as Amu emerged, 'Just wait!' He carefully placed the straight edges of the bits of clay against each other, and managed to get what looked like a corner.

'See, I've got two different sides, it looks like a long seal... it seems square, but much bigger than the ones I saw today,' he said triumphantly. 'This narrows it down, only a few like these have been made, most seals are rectangular in shape. I'm certain the seal makers will know this one.' The others agreed, although not quite knowing what he was talking about!

They decided they'd leave at once, so climbed over the wall, onto the tree and then jumped down lightly, onto the road. Mission accomplished!

Walking back to Lothal town, they saw the two-storeyed houses, which they now knew had their own wells. Xerxes told Amu, 'We are also going to have two-storeyed buildings in our village, in fact it's going to be a planned town! There is going to be a small crafts centre as well, that's why Kartik's father has come here. Anantpur always had good clay for the potters, and now they have found a stream with precious carnelian stones in it. Kartik's father will take on student artisans who want to train, they will live there and learn at the same time. Then people like my parents will continue with the sowing and ploughing, and the oxen will get water from the wells. My great grandfather came and buried all the wanderlust he felt in this village. '

He added, with a wry grin: 'Along with the seeds he sowed! He never ever left Anantpur after coming here. My parents never want to leave.'

'So what about cloth and wool and other things you need?' asked Amu curiously.

'Oh we'll get that from neighbouring villages, at least the bulk, the village elders have decided, some is woven in our village as well,' Xerxes replied.

Talk turned to Amu's father. 'I don't think I'll ever find him,' said Amu, wistfully.

'Maybe he's ill and lost,' reasoned Namami.

'Or maybe he's settled with another tribe,' said Xerxes. This was quite common—newcomers would often come into a village, like Xerxes's great grandfather, and would co exist peacefully alongside the others.

'No, my father would never do that. He'd come only for trading and meant to return,' Amu said angrily. 'My father was so devoted to the family... he never took other wives.' He said this with total conviction in his voice.

The others kept quiet; they could see why Amu had to believe there was some other explanation for his father's disappearance than the ones everyone offered him.

Kaveri broke the silence. 'Amu, about the bundle, if you hadn't been with us, we'd never have known,' she said.

The others looked at Amu, smiling gratefully, realizing they had found a great friend. Only Xerxes frowned again, his sense of worry returning.

'Let's keep walking,' he urged.

Soon they reached the busy market area, and decided to look for Kartik's and Kaveri's father again. 'Maybe we'll see Altairbhai there, and he'll be able to give us some news,' said Kartik, when they couldn't spot his father at the assigned area. Xerxes and Kartik left to look for Altairbhai, and Amu wandered off with the girls, who went to the stalls which had wares of interest for women. Here, they would look at jewellery, colourful rouge pots, and shawls.

What a babble of different dialects, and what a cheerful noise: babies gurgling, young girls and boys calling to each other, making for an atmosphere of gaiety and celebration. Everything was so colourful. Ladies displayed rush baskets, huge storage jars for grain, and other household items. There were toys: dolls and carts and animals made of clay and terracotta. Some animals moved along a string; Kaveri really loved those!

Namami looked at a lady who was wearing a deep red glowing necklace, with long, rectangular beads.

'I've never seen that. I would love to take that back for my mother.'

'Its carnelian, they get it from the river bed. And there's yellow jasper, like yours, but a darker shade,' piped up Kaveri, pointing to another lady as she showed off what she'd learnt at home.

'I'll barter my hair clasps and my terracotta toys. They are different from the ones here. Let me see, what shall I take?' Namami was equally thrilled at the prospect of shopping for jewellery.

Joker was sitting by the girls, playfully swiping at imaginary foes, when a real one appeared; a big dog came up to him and growled loudly. This made Joker turn tail, and he hurriedly went and hid behind Namami.

Namami shooed the big dog away and grinned. 'Not so brave, little one', she murmured, patting Joker gently, as she continued from stall to stall, Kaveri trailing behind her.

Joker darted away, all of a sudden, and turning round, Namami noticed that he was nowhere to be seen. She told Kaveri to go ahead and find Amu who had moved on ahead bored; she'd find that naughty dog and follow in just a few minutes and join them.

Things happen

Amu was walking around the market by himself, mulling over the meaning of the mystery map, when he saw the two men he'd seen at the big granary. He decided to follow them quietly, to try to find out more. They didn't know that he had any connection to his new friends. But he still had to lie low.

He trailed them, and they crossed the market and went to the open ground. Standing behind a thick, bushy shrub, he overheard them arguing, in the language they shared with him. He crouched behind a bush, and saw that they had spread the contents of their bundles around them.

'Hammur, you really bungled it, getting the child's bag,' one yelled.

'No, you did, Uri, getting off so quickly, I just picked the identical one. Why did we get off so fast? Why were you so frightened as soon as you heard the word robbery?' the other replied.

'This is Meluhha, not Mesopotamia, no one will punish you so severely for a robbery.'

Amu's heart was thudding wildly.

He heard the one called Uri's voice again: 'Hammur, we have got to find that girl.'

'I know her, I will recognize her because that dog is always with her. We'll track her down and change the bundles again,' said the one called Hammur.

'We need it so we can give the map to Sohrab, whoever he is, otherwise we won't get the other half. And that bulky figure... It is very important, though I don't know why. And what on earth are those small bits, they don't make any sense. Sonu who was with us when we robbed the temple didn't say what they were,' replied Uri.

'You are such a fool,' Hammur snapped. He sounded angry and irritated.

'I know... we have to join the maps... gold figures are... and only when we give that old figure will we get the map in exchange... then we'll be rich... go back to Mesopotamia, sell these, buy land, and keep slaves as well.' His voice had a satisfied, gloating note, but had dropped so Amu heard the conversation in bits, and not too clearly.

As both men fell silent, looking busy with their thoughts, Amu studied them intently. Both looked so ordinary, except the young one, who really did look girlish. No birthmarks or scars, he thought regretfully, what a pity. Then he saw it: the top of the boy's left ear had been sliced off at some point; it was flattish. It was only because he was at such an odd angle that Amu had noticed it. He stared at it with curiosity, wondering what could have happened to that ear.

The men gathered everything together and made for the market. Amu followed slowly, well behind them, so they wouldn't suspect that they were being followed. He had come a little closer to solving the mystery; he now knew what the two men were called and more worryingly, his suspicions were now backed by facts. He knew that his four friends were in danger, in particular little Kaveri! But she would be alright as long as the rest of them kept an eye on her. Uri and Hammur went around the various stalls looking for their quarry. Amu watched them from a distance, his eyes also moving to the lively bargaining that was going on at the ladies' stalls, further away.

Namami and Kaveri were at one such stall, and he saw Kaveri hold up her shell necklace and argue animatedly. He liked little Kaveri's spirit, and saw her dimple and two black plaits move sharply from side to side. Shaking her head vigorously, she appeared small and dark and full of vitality. She was refusing to part with something, he gathered! Then one plait went into her mouth, typically, and Amu couldn't help laughing.

But Namami had moved away in those two minutes AND Amu had missed something important!

He followed Kaveri, who wandered from stall to stall. She was safe, he could see. He called out,

'Kavi,' and waved to her. Some beautiful filigree necklaces caught his eye. How he would love to take those back for his mother… or the shining faience toys for his brothers and sisters. Till now he hadn't allowed himself to think of home and returning without his father, but now it seemed only too possible.

In the meanwhile, this is what had happened to Namami: she had seen Joker creeping through the bush and whistled, but he didn't turn around. The naughty puppy was following a smell he loved and he was going to wherever it was! She ran after him, and he shot off, till he was completely out of the market. He kept sniffing after the elusive scent, and wouldn't respond to her calls or whistles.

They crossed the hedges, which were almost like a boundary of the market. Very few people were around. In fact, it was rather lonely, as Namami realized belatedly. She reached some bushes, and bent down to peer through and see if Joker was on the other side.

Where is Namami?

'Joker!' she called. She was straightening up when a pair of hands clapped over her mouth and eyes. Her own hands were caught and held together tightly. A voice whispered in her ears, 'We want our things back. Make no noise and we'll let you go soon.'

Another voice, sharp and cutting, said curtly, 'The bag. We want it.' Namami froze. The truth hit her like a blow. In a flash she realized what had happened; these rough-sounding men were the two robbers! And she was cut off from everyone!

The men grabbed her bundle, flung a shawl round her and she was rolled into it like a parcel. They continued talking in Meluhhi, which they had used while threatening her. She heard a muffled voice say, 'Let's take it and go meet him... and then leave her a little further away, so it takes her a while to get back.'

'The cave?' asked the other voice, harsh and rough.

Namami thought hard and fast. She was trapped, no one knew where she was, certainly not Xerxes or Kartik. They'd keep looking in the market, but because it was so large, it would be ages before she'd be missed. Amu and Kaveri would think she had gone to the east gate on her own, to look for the boys. What a fool she'd been!

She could hardly breathe for fear. Carried like a sack of grain, lurching and swaying from side to side, she kept kicking, hoping they would stop and put her down, but the man just continued walking. He said, 'Make no noise and you will be safe, try to scream and we will harm you. You will be left far away.'

Her captor continued to walk for a good few minutes more, then put her down, saying to the other man angrily, 'You are of no use, hold the girl while I find the cave.' Quickly, Namami pushed away the shawl from her face, to try and see where she was, and managed to stand up, tottering slightly. She tried desperately to look around for some landmark. There was a guava tree behind her, at some distance; she was under a clump of babool trees with yellow flowers, and some orange marigolds flowered near these trees; no other landmark.

'Look she's got up! Why couldn't you keep hold of her more tightly?' The first man exclaimed in annoyance, and Namami saw only that he was large and angry looking, before the second man pinned her arms behind her, pulled the shawl over her head, and threw her over his shoulder again. After walking for a few minutes, he stooped, stumbled a few paces, and put her down. They were in a cave-like place, she could sense, dim and quiet in a very scary way.

The whole mela, the market, Kartik, Kaveri, Xerxes, and Amu seemed to belong to another world.

Where was Joker? She was so alone. Why wasn't he following her?

The men pushed her further inside the cave, roughly.

'There is a passage here, crawl through and you will come out,' said one. 'Walk around the hill and you will come to the river. Keep to the left bank and you will reach the mela ground. See, that side… '

'You fool, we have brought her to the wrong cave, there is no passage out from here, it's a blank wall, a dead end!' cried the other, his voice sharp with irritation. 'And we can't take her with us. There is no way out. We'll have to take her somewhere else.'

'No, let's hurry, we've got to get that other half. Let her wait here alone,' said the first man cruelly. 'Here you,' he addressed Namami, 'Sit down quietly and we'll be back soon. And don't you dare shout for anyone, no one can hear you, anyway.'

Namami believed this. She kept quiet, not knowing what to do.

The men left, and suddenly it was darker; they had blocked the entrance with a big rock!

Namami shouted in fear, and tried to move the rock, but to no avail; it was too heavy for her and wouldn't budge.

In the meanwhile, Joker, had run off, following a scent he loved: food. He'd heard Namami call for him, but he'd ignored her, having more interesting thoughts on his mind. He'd return to his beloved mistress after eating.

And Kaveri, still on her own in the ladies' stalls, finally looked around. Where were Namami and Joker?

Just when she was starting to get worried, Amu Darya came up to her and smiled in his reassuring way. But Kaveri was distracted and anxious and it showed; Amu's expression changed.

'Why, Kaveri, what's wrong? Why are you looking troubled? And where are Nami and Joker?'

'Both have vanished, Joker ran off and wouldn't come to us, so Nami ran after him,' replied Kaveri.

'But I saw her, just a little while ago. She must be around. After you both wandered off, I went to the crafts corner, and then I saw that same monkey. See, he took those bangles and wore them and scampered away. There he is!' Both of them started laughing, watching the monkey's antics.

Amu was sure Namami had got caught up at one of the stalls, and decided they'd wait at the same place in case she came. Five minutes, then ten, still no sign of her. They became impatient.

She must be in her favourite herb corner, they thought.

'I'm scared,' admitted the usually bold Kaveri, finally, clutching Amu's arm.

Amu could see she was upset, but thought that she was imagining the worst in her excitement. The lively little girl had an overactive imagination and often reacted quickly to things, frightening herself unneccessarily, in the bargain.

'Nami never ever leaves me alone, that's why my mother likes us to go together. Maybe she is with Xerxes and Kartik, and they have found my father... ' she trailed off hopefully.

They looked around the marketplace. Kaveri saw the lady who had given them the 'thalipeeth', doing brisk business with her food stall. 'Please, Ma,' she asked her politely, 'have you seen the other girl who was with us, Nami, the tall girl? We can't see her anywhere.'

'No, I haven't seen her,' the lady replied. 'Why don't you go to the pottery side, she said earlier she liked the red vase with the black border of deer on it. She wanted to take that for her mother, she told me.'

Joker came prancing up just then, looking a real clown with one ear up and one ear down over his eye. His tail wagged ridiculously, and he seemed to be laughing.

'He's eaten something. You naughty dog, you've stolen fish, and I can smell it,' scolded Kaveri, as she bent down to pat him. But as Joker had no idea what 'stolen' meant, he just wagged his tail even more,said 'Woof, woof', and licked Kaveri's toes. He was smart enough to know this always made her laugh! He ran around them, darted ahead, turned around, came back, and barked, as if asking 'Where is my Nami?'

'Joker, where is Nami? Do you know?' asked Kaveri. Of course Joker couldn't understand a word, but he cocked up his ears at the name 'Nami'.

Kaveri told Amu urgently, 'Let's look for her, she has to be somewhere close-by.'

They started walking, and again Joker appeared and pulled at Kaveri's skirt, almost dragging her. He was sniffing the ground, then he turned and took them to where Kaveri had been standing earlier, when she had realized she was alone. He kept sniffing, ran ahead, and stood near the bushes, barking at Kaveri and Amu, clearly saying 'Come on, follow me... What are you waiting for?'

'He's got her scent!' exclaimed Amu Darya, thankfully. 'What a relief. We'll find her soon.' But once they were in the open maidan bordering the market, there was still no sign of her! There were a few people around, mainly under shady mango trees. It was so, so, hot; most people were still resting. There was a rishi under a peepul tree, meditating, but they knew it was no use disturbing him; he didn't even notice them.

Joker kept going, sniffing the ground. Suddenly he went round and round in a circle, till Kaveri thought she would scream. Her patience was really at an end, and she was close to tears.

Amu watched Joker intently. He seemed to give up. He just sat and scratched himself vigorously. Then, he retreated a little and started giving short excited yaps. 'He's got something, some scent, let's see what he does,' shouted Amu.

Joker raced ahead, in the direction of the small hillocks which had the rock base they had noticed whilst coming. Why would Namami have gone so far? Both Amu and Kaveri were really worried by now.

Joker stopped under the babool trees, right near the orange flowers, sniffed and gave a quick bark, and set off, sniffing and giving small barks as if saying 'Follow me, I'll find my Nami.'

'He knows where Namami is!' They were sure she was close-by.

'Nami, Nami,' they kept calling, more cheerful now, but still uncertain. There were many small shrubs there, so she could be anywhere, they thought. Peering into the shrubbery, they were lost for a minute.

Then they turned around: Joker had vanished.

Now Amu and Kaveri kept yelling out for Joker as well as for Namami. Puzzled, but quite sure he would lead them to Namami, they walked back towards the hillocks where they'd last spotted him.

'This is no time for hide and seek,' said Kaveri, crossly. Amu nodded silently. Yes, this was no time for games.

What had happened to Namami?

Meanwhile, what HAD happened to Namami?

When the two men left, saying they would be back soon to let her out, Namami was left alone, terrified. Her bundle! It was with them! Thankfully, they had been in too much of a hurry to open it. Little did they know that they had got the wrong person!

She remembered how Joker had been with Kaveri for part of the ride. 'They must have thought Joker was always with Kaveri, And that I am actually her!' she thought.

Now she had to wait for them, shut up inside a dark cave.

'They will be so angry when they will discover their mistake. I don't know what they'll do with me when they return. And if I tell them, they'll know we've found the map. They'll return soon, I have to think of something. I have to hide, but where?' Namami said all of this aloud, to delay the great fear which was overtaking her.

Thinking quickly, and with her heart hammering away, she looked around at the semi-darkness. It seemed to engulf her completely.

'Where? What? How?' these thoughts raced through her head. 'If only Joker was me... ' Her knees felt like jelly, and she thought she couldn't move another step.

She stood there, rubbing her shoulder, which felt sore. The man had clamped his hand over her mouth, which was now dry and parched, and he had been very rough when he pinned her arms behind her; they throbbed with pain as well. She felt bruised and shaken, and very, very alone.

Namami tried pushing the rock, but it was big and heavy and wouldn't budge an inch. There was a small gap at the side, but it was far too small for her to crawl through. Luckily, it let in some dim light.

She decided to go to the end of the cave and sit, resting her sore back and aching arms, and felt her way there slowly.

'It should end soon, a rock wall should be somewhere here,' she thought, as she banged her head on the sloping ceiling. The left hand side of the wall felt hard and rocky, but surprisingly the right side felt smoother as she trailed her hand across it. She sat down in despair, then got up again, urgency lending her speed.

She scraped her hand on the rocky wall near her, and nearly fell. Then, getting up, she started moving, determinedly, towards the other end of the cave. But her feet and hands felt only air around them, not the solid end as she expected. The ceiling was lower and she had to now crawl on her hands and feet. And all the time she moved further and further away from the entrance.

A shiver of fear ran down her spine. What was down this passage, and how big was it? She tried to stand, but oww, her head hit the roof of rock above her with a bang! Should she stay where she was, or should she go ahead and hide from the men, and hope they wouldn't find her? She made up her mind and began to crawl again, edging her way forward slowly. Anything was better than facing the two men's wrath when they returned empty-handed.

She began to feel an air current as she worked her way to the back of the cave. 'This is fresh air,' she thought, 'so it means there is a way out—but I've been crawling and crawling, and it seems to go on and on. Is this a tunnel? It's become so dark now, I can hardly see. I just hope there aren't any bats or spiders.' She shuddered; she was petrified of spiders.

Namami touched her amulet, and called to the spirits of the air and the sun to protect her. Her mother had given her this amulet to ward off bad luck and to protect her, and she never took it off. Now she held onto it tightly, putting all her faith in the elements they worshipped.

Her thoughts were dancing madly in her head, but just touching her dark yellow jasper stone calmed her.

Every thing she had learnt with her parents whilst searching for rare herbs and plants helped her now. 'I have to get out,' she thought. Even in her terrified state of mind, she had to admit to herself that it was a little better than some of the expeditions on which she had been with her father! Once, in search of a rare plant which grew in a particular valley, they had had to cross through just such a passage, but a more nerve racking one, as they'd crossed a long, narrow ledge with water flowing beneath them.

She remembered her father saying, 'Take a deep, deep breath always. Never ever rush. Breathing slowly and deeply always helps to calm and still the mind, and then you can think clearly.' How she missed him now. And Xerxes, Kartik, and Kaveri.

She stopped and did a pranayam for a precious few minutes. It felt like two hours to her overstretched imagination.

'I'll keep moving forward and think of all the beautiful flowers I have ever seen, and then the butterflies,' she decided. She continued moving for a while, then suddenly felt the narrow tunnel widen. 'I'm so cramped, maybe I'll be able to sit for a minute. Let me try,' she told herself.

To her delight and relief, she found the roof was higher, and that she could now sit up. She sat for a minute, and then began to crawl again.

'The air is different now, definitely fresher—it's moving. A breeze? But how could that be? Maybe I'm near some hole which leads outside.'

Sure enough, she was through the passage. Grazed, cut, scratched, and bleeding on her knees and hands and elbows, trembling with exhaustion and fear: but she was out!!

Freedom

Namami crawled out and looked around. She was completely lost. Nothing looked familiar. She started walking towards something that glistened in the distance—the river.

'If I follow it, I'll get close to the field with the rishis and tents and people preparing for the Surya Mela; the grand prayers are in a few days' time,' she thought.

She was so relieved that in spite of her bleeding knees and elbows, and smarting wrists, she started running. She kept turning, every few minutes, fearing the men would find her. But no one was there. There was total, eerie silence. This place was deserted.

How she longed for the buzz of the market with its groups of people, tiny stalls of food, shrill cries of children, the sounds of different dialects and the air of activity. This isolated spot held only terror for her, now.

She was thirsty and exhausted by the long crawl. The terror of the men finding her haunted her. She saw a peepul tree ahead and ran to it. Some monkeys were swinging from the banyan tree right next to it. She laughed, and felt better. She bowed down to pray, as peepul trees were sacred, and many prayers and rituals were conducted around it.

'Oh spirit of the sacred tree, spirits of the air and the sun, please help me to find my way. I have to find the others.'

She got up quickly as she looked at the distant water, and set off towards it. Once she reached the banks of the stream and followed it, she knew she would reach the field near the market. She walked for at least fifteen minutes, and realized she'd soon be at the river. Her fear receded; there were so many trees—some cover at last—and there were a few tied up oxen and a few goats grazing. Now she could hide again if needed.

She reached the low bank of the river, and looking at the clean, sparkling water, bent down to drink it. She cupped her hands and drank deeply, till her thirst was quenched. Refreshed, she set off again, but there were no people, no boats. 'It looks much smaller now that I am close to it,' she thought, looking at the river, and kept walking, hoping to see someone.

Tired and puzzled, it dawned on her that she might have walked away from the market instead of towards it. She sat down and looked around, completely disheartened. 'All that walking was in vain, and maybe I've gone farther away from the others,' she thought, full of despair. 'What if the men come to look for me and I walk right into them?'

Then, sitting with her head in her hands, on the verge of tears, she suddenly heard a bark she knew all too well. And she had never been so glad to hear it!

'Joker, here, Joker!' she shouted, standing up, laughing and utterly delighted. Her beloved Joker had come for her. He reached her and lick, lick, lick, he jumped up and she thought she'd need a towel! He was so happy that he rolled and pranced around her. He had found her; his nose had led him to her. And he knew the way back!

Clever Joker had squeezed through a tiny opening near the big rock, which had blocked the entrance. He had followed Namami's trail from where the men had set her down, near the babool trees. Then, he had single-mindedly followed her scent, also recognizing another scent—the men's. On entering the cave, he had picked up her scent again; his beloved Namami's familiar smell. She was somewhere nearby! Putting his little nose to the ground, the remarkable little dog had followed her crawling progress, step for step; all the way out and to the river he had run, eager to see his mistress.

What hugs he got now! Namami held him to her, and finally sobbed, all her pent up emotions finally breaking free. Her prayers to all the spirits had been answered. She had a friend with her again.

She touched the lucky charm she wore at her neck, a jasper gem and a beautifully carved steatite seal, which bore the sun and water and a unicorn; she had been protected all through that narrow, low passage! She gave thanks to the spirits for her safety.

Joker is smart

Joker tugged and tugged at Namami's robe, walked away and came back again. 'You want me to follow you, Joker?' she asked, a little puzzled. After all, Joker had not been with her for all that long, though she felt she'd known him for ever. Again, Joker pulled hard and this time she decided to leave everything to him. In any case, she hadn't been so clever today!

Joker took her in the direction opposite to where she'd been going. They had been walking for ten minutes when Namami saw water again. As they neared the river bank, she saw the difference at once. They were near the river Pavitra; she could recognize it.

This was wider, and deeper, and darker. There were little paths, bordered by boulders, leading to the river, and there were also small bathing ghats and steps at various points, where pious persons were already meditating. Small boats took people further down the river. Namami now knew they were going in the correct direction. But, for the same reason, she was also frightened—suppose the two men saw her? Her heart continued to beat like a drum.

'If they ask me, I'll say that I don't know any thing about it nor do the others. I'll pretend to be totally bewildered about the bag. I'll keep saying, "But you said you took my bag by mistake; it's still with me... I don't know what you are talking about." '

Lost in thought, Namami felt a sharp twinge of pain just then; she hadn't known how hard she had been biting her nails, till she had hurt her finger just now! She gave a small smile when she thought of Kaveri teasing her about her nailbiting. 'How right she was, I haven't lost my habit as yet! But I bite only these last two nails now,' she consoled herself. Her mind was a jumble of thoughts, flowing in all directions.

Namami and Joker kept walking, keeping close to the riverside. As long as they stayed near it, they'd eventually reach the marketplace. Joker was running ahead; but he'd wait, as though telling her that he wouldn't leave her, turn his head and give a short bark every few moments, as if saying, 'You are taking too long.' Namami hurried, but she was tired and her legs took twice as long as usual to move. Then, she thought of the wrath of the two men and fear lent her speed immediately.

As she scurried along, she noticed more activity, and more people. If she spotted the men now, she could create a commotion and call for help, she thought, reassured.

Finally, the party of two reached the market, but from a different side. Namami glanced around quickly, checking if Kartik or Kaveri or Xerxes were close-by. All she could see were strangers who had come for the mela. Then, she looked around hopefully to check if Kaveri's father had come, and was sitting with his pots and various wares, but couldn't see him either.

She sniffed the now familiar aroma of the market's different foods. Joker had slowed down now and seemed very satisfied with himself, nose pointing to the meats, saying, 'I deserve those, don't you think?' She bent down, patted him, and whispered, 'Joker you shall have everything you want.' Hearing music nearby, lovely, ordinary sounds, she at once felt safe and better.

She decided to go to the corner with all the ladies' stalls. Maybe... yes, yes, YES! Right back at that same stall she'd last visited, were Amu Darya and Kaveri. She had never felt happier seeing her friends.

Running to them, Joker right behind her, she yelled out, 'Amu! Kaveri, Kaveri!'

The two spotted her, and ran towards her, meeting her halfway, both with a relieved smile on their faces.

'Nami, where *were* you?' shouted Kaveri, who was both relieved and happy to see that her friend had returned. 'Where were you? We searched and searched for you.'

Namami smiled weakly, still shaken, and Kaveri hugged her over and over again. Amu stood by the two protectively, Joker dancing around the little group, and Amu laughed at the picture they made.

But now Amu and Kaveri could see, as they looked closely at Namami's face, that something terribly unpleasant had happened. Amu suggested gently, 'Let's find somewhere quiet to sit.'

'No, no,' remonstrated Namami, very vehemently. She wanted to stick to crowds for a while, understandably. So the three plonked themselves down close-by, and Namami told them everything that had happened, all the horrible events.

Amu and Kaveri were horrified and shocked to think that Namami had been captured and hidden away so easily. They had never ever come across something like this. And how cruel the men had been: they shuddered, thinking of the ordeal Namami had gone through. Kaveri told her how they'd searched and searched, trying to find her.

Amu went quiet. On the ship coming here, he had grown up a lot and seen and heard things meant for more grown-up ears. He knew that Namami had got off lightly.

'Clever Joker! Clever boy!' How they praised and made a fuss of the little puppy, who wagged his tail as they petted him! How they praised

Namami, for being so brave and escaping through that dark passage, with nothing but strength of mind to guide her!

'You have no idea how scared I was. How I wished I hadn't left this marketplace. Those men came up behind me so quietly and silently, I didn't get a chance to scream,' she told them.

'They really want the bag badly,' mused Amu, looking alarmed and trying not to show it.

'They'll come looking for us now.'

'Maybe we should say we threw it away and that anyone could have picked it up,' said Kaveri, hopefully.

'One thing's for sure: no one is to go alone anywhere now,' said Amu firmly. He was one of them now, and the girls agreed, nodding.

Amu then told them what he'd heard the men saying earlier. A shiver ran down Namami's spine. Adventure this was, exciting and so different from anything that had ever happened to them before—but most unpleasant. What unlawful things were happening? Would they ever know?

'It's the stolen treasure. It must be! The clues in our bag must lead to the stolen treasures of Mohenjo-daro. That's what they needed—the map! By the spirits, this is dangerous. We have never come across anything like this,' said Namami.

'Maybe we should bring the packet back and find those men and just give it to them…,' started Kaveri, eyes dark with fear. 'Then we'll be rid of them.' She was still shocked about all that Namami had gone through.

'We'll do no such thing!' Namami and Amu turned on her indignantly.

'You don't think I went through that horrifying time to hand over something that may lead us to the precious treasures and figures of the priest-king? They belonged to the whole of Mohenjo-daro and are tied with our own honour as well,' Namami told Kaveri, firmly but gently.

Their clans placed great value on honour, fair play, and justice. So did Amu's, and the punishment for not observing these laws was severe.

'Yes, but you may never have come out from there, how would we have ever found you?' cried Kaveri, her face small with distress.

'Joker would have brought you to me,' said Namami, airily. Because she was safe now, she could afford to act daring, though her grazes and cuts still stung. The first thing she had done was to wash them in the cold river water and dry them, but still...

'Nothing like this has been heard of before in Mesopotamia. The law is so strict that everyone is afraid to break it,' declared Amu. 'In our land, if we call someone a thief, we have to prove that he is a thief, otherwise we are punished.'

'Nor have we ever heard of such a thing. I wonder what will happen now,' said Namami, with a shudder.

'Why haven't Kartik and Xerxes come till now? And my father?' squeaked Kaveri, looking worried.

All she wanted was to see her father and brother.

Now that they'd seen Namami's grazed and bleeding knuckles, her torn and dirty robe, she had a sense of the danger of their situation. She wondered what she would have done in Namami's place. They just couldn't understand this kind of behaviour.

They were such a gentle, peace loving people. At home, they led such a quiet life, and self-defence was the only form of combat taught. They spent more time on finer pursuits. Of course, fear of wild animals was very real, so shooting bows and arrows using sharpened sticks in defence, and practising their aim for hunting was encouraged and taught; the boys hunted. Kaveri sighed and thought about their safe, secure life at home, feeling quite homesick.

The sun was setting now, a red orb; long shadows were beginning to show everywhere. Amu saw that the girls were both missing the comfort of home, and began to tell them about the sunsets at sea, their glorious colours of orange and ruby red, and the blue sea turning to purple and then darkening to black. A change of topic would be good for the little girl who had just got the scare of her life.

Xerxes and Kartik wait for Appa

In the meanwhile, hours earlier, Xerxes and Kartik had walked to the small granary, hoping they would meet Kartik's father; but their efforts were in vain. They joked and chattered as usual, but they were both bothered about the way they had taken and hidden something which didn't belong to them. The elders back home certainly wouldn't have approved their act. But then again, the elders weren't at the mela, stranded without Appa, with strange men in search of them. And sacred treasures usually hadn't been stolen from the high priest! 'These are desperate times,' Xerxes announced—rather self-evidently, Kartik thought!—'and they call for desperate measures.'

'Did you get that from your father?' Kartik teased. Xerxes hit him on the head, laughing.

They grew serious again when they remembered the details of the robbery at Mohenjo-daro.

How they wished Kartik's father would arrive. The idea of having an adventure, like the stories they heard, was wonderful, but they could have asked for Appa's advice, or just handed the problem over to him, which was less exciting, but probably the right thing to do, they knew.

At the same time, they both wanted to solve the mystery of the missing treasure. Imagine if they found it! What pride the whole village would feel! Perhaps the head of their village would be called to Mohenjo-daro!

They began to wonder what could have held Appa up. Losing a wheel was common. Surely an ox-cart didn't take so long to repair? Were the others from Anantpur alright? Was Appa alright? They'd left him alone, after all. But it had been very safe, where he was. Maybe they'd find him at the gate right now, talking and laughing and waiting to ask them why *they* were late!

They neared the same small granary they'd been at yesterday, and walked through its long passages. There, they bumped into Altairbhai again.

'Altairbhai, have you seen Appa? Has he passed by?' asked Kartik, after greeting the tall man. He and Xerxes looked at each other; they had wondered earlier if they should take their secret to someone else—some other grown-up—to decide what they should do. But they were sure Appa would be here any time now, and didn't want to get anyone else involved. They liked Altairbhai, but didn't know him well enough to confide in him; not only would they have to tell him they had hidden stolen property, he would perhaps decide to take over. They were quite certain they would solve this all on their own.

Altairbhai shook his head. 'And where are the girls?' he asked.

'They are waiting in the market, where my father will sell his wares once he's here,' replied Kartik.

'But hasn't he reached already? That's strange, it wasn't so far away that his cart broke down,' Altairbhai told them, looking concerned.

'That's what we felt, I'm getting worried... I hope a tiger or wild boar hasn't wandered out of the jungle,' added Kartik, becoming more anxious, hearing the worry in Altairbhai's voice.

Xerxes voted for action, as always. 'Let's look around very carefully and ask people, maybe someone has seen him... in any case I'm sure Appa will turn up here soon.'

They bade farewell to Altairbhai and walked through the granary, hoping they would bump into Appa any moment. After an hour, they debated whether to return to the market. The golden evening air was slowly turning to dusk, and the air was much cooler now.

'Appa wouldn't expect us to wait here for so long... let's go,' Kartik finally told Xerxes, worry showing on his face. 'We'll be with the girls, all together, at least.'

As they set out, they were joined by the boy they'd seen earlier, doing tricks with the same monkey who now sat on his shoulder. He was walking the same way, and called out to them, saying 'Hey, wait!' They turned to greet him, happy to have company, and he introduced himself: 'I am Shyon, from Mayurpur.'

They did the customary open-palmed greeting, introduced themselves, and began to chat.

'Your monkey is really clever. What's his name? Can he do any tricks?' asked Xerxes.

'Of course he can, and his name is Binku. He's trying to juggle, like me, and he can give you our greeting!' he grinned.

'Binku,' he ordered, 'show them how we say "I come to you in peace" when we meet new people.'

And Binku the monkey promptly put out his hands, opened his tiny little palms, and bent his head!

'Binku, say you are sorry,' cajoled Shyon, slyly holding a small fruit in his hand.

Binku's eyes shone and he obliged at once. He covered his eyes with one hand, bent his head down (peeping naughtily through his fingers, though!) and with his free hand gently slapped himself, making a sad, crooning sound. He did sound sorry!

The boys burst out laughing and got him to act out some more lines. Shyon started singing a catchy song, and Binku did a funny little dance, keeping perfect time to the rhythym: out came a paw, up went his leg, he twirled around, skipped and put out his paws again.

'He's as good as any performer!' exclaimed Xerxes.

Binku ended by clapping, looking very pleased with himself. Jibbering away, the monkey finally sprang onto Shyon's shoulder. The boys laughed, and told Shyon how they had made friends with a boy who came from a land without monkeys!

'Binku would certainly be a hit there!' said Shyon, shouting with laughter.

They walked on, passing two men who asked the way to the small granary. Then, a little behind them, huffing and puffing, appeared an elderly lady, struggling under the weight of the bundle she was carrying. She was short and round, with wispy grey hair.

'Grandma! Give that to us. We'll help you,' offered Xerxes gently.

Only then they noticed the baby in the shawl, hung on the woman's back in a sling-like fashion.

'My granddaughter. I have to go to the market and I seem to have got lost. Someone said it would take an hour. I am so tired now,' sighed the old lady.

'No Grandma, we know a short cut and we'll be there very soon,' replied the boys.

'If we don't have to stop and give directions to the small granary, or the dockyard, or to Lothal town!' joked Kartik.

'Maybe,' laughed Xerxes, 'we have a sign around our necks saying "Guide to Lothal" and that's why each one feels we'll send them the right way!'

Walking with the old lady, telling her about the new foods they had eaten in the market, they saw a tall man, striding along fast. When he neared them, Xerxes winked at Kartik and whispered to him, 'I bet he'll ask us the way to the market, or the granary.'

Sure enough, the stranger came up to them, and all four went through the ritual greeting.

He was young and had a marked limp. 'Could you tell me the way to the dockyard? I am in a hurry.'

'Carry on straight, then turn right and keep walking, there is a long brick wall, when you reach the end you will see it,' said Xerxes confidently.

'How much longer?' asked Shyon, who was openly laughing and enjoying what he called the guided tour the boys were giving strangers.

Grandma appeared tired now. 'We'll soon be at the market, Grandma, and now no one will come to ask us the way,' said Xerxes, with a grin.

But he was wrong. 'Here's one more,' grinned Shyon, poking Kartik in the ribs.

A man came up ahead of them, hurrying, having obviously just reached Lothal, as he still carried a big bundle on his back. Speaking in a slightly different accent, he said, 'I am Sohrab, and I come in peace. Do you know where the big granary is? I am very late. I have to meet a couple of men there, and I don't want to waste my time searching. Could you help me?'

They looked at him. He looked like a foreigner although he was dressed like them. He was fair, with light coloured eyes and had reddish hair, unusual for these parts. He had a long beard, which partly hid his face—which was pleasant-looking—and a ready smile, his eyes crinkling up when he smiled. His most distinguishing feature on his was face was a long, livid scar that ran along his forehead.

The boys liked him at once. 'Walk till you come to a long road—there is a thick, fortressed wall made of baked bricks, turn left and you will be at the west gate, turn right from there. You will see the warehouse. That is the shortest way.'

'There is so much activity as they are expecting a boat from Mesopotamia. There was a boat from Dilmun, they told us this morning,' Xerxes elaborated, wondering if the stranger was a seafarer.

The man looked thoughtful. 'I have a parcel to go to Dilmun. I am from Dholavira. My grateful thanks, young lads.' He bowed his head, opened his palms wide, and the boys did likewise, immediately; the man seemed to command respect.

After he had overtaken them, all of them, including Grandma, burst out laughing. 'You boys are real guides. Telling one person where the warehouse is, and giving the other a shortcut to the granary,' she exclaimed.

The boys didn't realize why everyone came to them for directions; they had bright, open faces, and seemed friendly and capable.

They arrived at the market soon, and looked for the girls. 'We'll have to tell them Appa hasn't come,' murmured Kartik, with a frown.

Both boys were increasingly uneasy about the strange package that had so changed things. Suppose Appa got angry and said it was none of their business; why had they interfered? Little did they know that their adventure had just become more dangerous.

All together again

Xerxes and Kartik bid Grandma goodbye, and when Shyon's monkey started to chatter excitedly and point at a group of people, it was time to take leave of their newfound friend as well. 'Those are some people from my village, he knows them,' grinned Shyon. He waved at them as he walked away.

The boys walked round the market, checking each spot to see if the girls were there. They found Amu Darya first, and then saw Namami and Kaveri. Kaveri looked at them, questioningly.

'No, Kavi, Appa hasn't come,' said Kartik, shaking his head regretfully.

It was only then that he noticed Namami's slightly wild look, though she had tried to tidy up. There were brown smudges on her face, which looked pale and wan. Her clothes looked a little grimy, and her hair was unruly, with cobwebs in it. And there was still fear in her eyes. Everyone spoke together, at the same time. Only Kaveri's shrill tone outdid the others.

Finally Amu managed to tell them clearly what had happened, adding in his discoveries as well.

Kartik and Xerxes were absolutely astounded. That anyone would *kidnap* one of them, and that too in broad daylight!

'This is dangerous!' exclaimed Xerxes, aghast. 'Appa left me in charge, I have to protect you girls.'

'Look, Xerxes, let's just get rid of this bag. It's big trouble,' said Kartik, wildly. He had been carrying the bag around these last few hours, and thinking of Namami's ordeal, now looked at it with distaste. We don't want the girls to be at the receiving end of their wrath.

'No, Kartik, we don't know what other evidence they will provide, or what importance those things may have. I'll put it in my other bundle,' said Amu calmly, realizing that this wouldn't solve the bigger problem; the two men were now clearly after them. He took the bag from the smaller boy and put it into his own bundle.

'You will have to disguise yourself, so no one will recognize you.' Xerxes told Namami, pulling himself together. 'Let me go get something for you from that stall over there.'

'Wait, take this turquoise and use it for Nami,' said Amu.

Xerxes and Kartik looked at Amu Darya, truly touched. It was really very generous of him to sacrifice his stone for a new friend who was in danger. After all, he had his own quest, the one he had come all the way from Mesopotamia for. He needed all he had, to barter, eat, and live here while he was still searching for his father. Even now, Amu's eyes kept darting around to see if his father was there. Being with the others had given him hope again.

They went and got the things they wanted: new haldi coloured and red clothes , along with a hair clasp only older women used, which they had seen in the upper town.

'Nami, use the shawl we have got and cover your shoulders. Partly cover your face and head, and let it drape around your waist, tuck it in there, like the lady there,' said Kartik, pointing to a lady talking to a little girl.

'And hurry and change into these clothes, and get Kaveri to help you with a different hair style... like the lady there,' said Kartik, pointing to a woman with a nice looking bun. 'We don't want those men to recognize you. We'll tie a string to Joker and keep him close to us.'

Both the girls looked at the lady and burst out laughing. They couldn't imagine Namami with such an elaborate hairstyle. It would take much time and patience to curl, plait, and coil hair high up on the head, or to shape it into the beehive type of hair-do that was so admired by older women here.

'That'll take us hours! We'll do what Amma does, just coil it and keep it up with a hair clasp, or plait it and wind it around my head,' said Namami with a laugh. 'But I really needed a change, so these new clothes are a great idea.

I'll look different and feel better, I'm so sticky and dirty.' She trembled, remembering her narrow escape.

Kaveri took her to the well close-by, and both used a copious amount of water to freshen up.

Namami hastily changed, then plaited, coiled, and shaped her long hair into a bun on the top of her head. Transformed, she returned to the others. Grandly, she twirled around, feeling much better, now that she was clean and all dolled up.

'Nami, you look so different! So grown up! And not at all like our Nami!' exclaimed Xerxes. Both Amu and Kartik nodded their heads in agreement.

She did look very grown up, and completely different; very elegant, with her new clothes and coiled hair, and certainly felt calmer and more composed. Of course, being all together again contributed much to this!

'Those men!' she muttered with a flash of irritation. 'They have taken my bag. I had my bone needles and thread; Amma wouldn't let me take the bronze needles. I could have mended my skirt.'

'Yes, she's back to normal!' quipped Xerxes, dodging Namami's swift hands as they reached for his ear.

'They will see Joker and recognize us,' murmured Kartik, scratching his head. Then, finding a solution, he added, 'I know, we'll pretend we are looking for Nami if they see us. Now, let's try and find Shyon, the boy with the monkey and stay with him.'

The five moved on through the marketplace. At his urging, Amu Darya began telling Xerxes about nights at sea. 'When the moon is at its fullest, the water looks first purple and then black, and you can see the silver gleam of the moonlight on the water, and the stars so bright, the soft cool, almost cold breeze and the salt tang in the air just makes you think of another secret world,' he told an envious Xerxes, who was drinking this all in with a rapt and dreamy expression.

'Here, come down to earth, forget your sea,' shouted Kartik, jolting Xerxes out of his reverie. 'We have to make sure we're close to the rest of the crowd, and mingle.'

The sun was setting fast, and soon shadows would form stark silhouettes against the orange glow from the west. This reminded Amu Darya of the heartstoppingly beautiful sunsets at sea, and he tried to describe this to the others, as they moved through the crowd. As twilight turned to darkness, there were tiny fireflies in the distance, flickering like tiny fairy lamps. Kaveri called them mini floating stars!

They felt much safer now, with so many people around. The friendly darkness would hide them from those evil men.

Groups of people had lit small fires, and were sitting around them. People were eating, chatting, and eagerly waiting for the river caravan from the north east. The Ganga people they were called, though the river they came from was not the Ganga, but another one. To the people in the west, however, all of the east was 'Gangaland'! They brought camphor, spices, timber, and muslin, which were sent to far off shores like Amu's. Timber was used for roofs both in Meluhha and Mespotamia.

A commotion broke out suddenly. A goat and her kid had gone and bumped into a potter's stall, bleating and baa-ing, kicking his wares, and then being chased and caught by the irate owner, who was shouting at them at the top of his voice. Add to that the stall owner's threats and swears and curses, and there was a complete hullabaloo! Finally, it was decided that the potter would get a goat in exchange for the lost clay pots and jars; this with a lot of mediation from spectators, who laughed at the little mishap, as it looked so comical.

The children had some snacks, which Kartik had got from the marketplace, and looked for a place to settle and munch on them, while watching the boats come in, like everyone around them. True, they now felt safer, but they still felt doubtful.

'There will be too few people at the small warehouse,' decided Xerxes, 'for it to be safe.'

'Let's move with the crowd and go near the riverside,' suggested Kartik. It would be just crowded enough there. 'No one can harm us then. But we have to stay together, in pairs. Amu Darya, you too—we can't take chances, they may have seen you talk to us.'

'Hey, walk faster, the boat caravan is coming,' squealed an excited Kaveri.

The children stayed close to a group of five men who looked friendly and 'normal', as Kaveri put it. They were chatting in a mild, jocular manner, as the village folk did at home. Having found their spot by the riverside, close to this group, they made themselves comfortable. The delicate fragrance of the raat-ki-rani creeper filled the air, as the dainty buds opened into fragile star shapes nearby.

'We don't have these sweet smelling flowers in our land,' Amu told the rest in wonder.

Word had spread quickly. It was a sight worth waiting for! No boats from the east, Gangaland, ever came singly—there were at least six in each lot. The hill people came with them, as well the traders from Varanasi. It was a beautiful sight. The river Pavitra now looked absolutely transformed.

The boats had small flame torches, which lit up the scene. The outlines of the boats looked spectacular, and they streamed in gracefully, in fives and sixes. Lot after lot came to the landing stage, and there they were assisted as they unloaded. Some continued further downstream.

The children watched, round-eyed and enchanted, drinking in all the romance.

'Imagine how they have come... imagine the sandalwood and the fine cloth. The different colours, the different clothes.' Everything was new and astonishing to the children who had never before left their village.

Amu Darya began to sing softly as he watched, and though the others couldn't understand the words, it sounded thrilling. He told them his song's meaning. It was the 'Song of Gilgamesh', which he'd sung to the crew during his long passage to Meluhha, and he told them it's story—of a warrior king who wanted to be immortal, of his deeds brave and valorous. The king had fought two lions, and tamed some, and even carried one cub as a pet in his arms.

It was now late, and Kaveri yawned. This set off the whole lot. Namami could barely keep her eyes open. Her ordeal had left her more exhausted than she could understand or would admit. But Kartik noticed her weariness and decided they would return to the small granary where they had slept the night before.

By the time they arrived, the air had become still. The sky was overcast with heavy dark clouds. 'A storm,' observed Amu, remembering his days at sea.

Almost immediately, there was a loud thunder, and all the children raced to the doorway again. They wanted to watch this storm. Lightning ripped the sky in two at that moment; and then there was the harsh sound of cascading rain.

Kaveri's expressive little face reflected her wonder as she enjoyed the show. Watching the display of emotions that chased across her face, Amu couldn't help laughing. She gave him a sudden grin.

'Kavi, its ok for you, you are in a nice sheltered place, so you can see the beauty of the storm. Think, if you were at sea, or on the river, and your boat was rocked and thrown around by choppy waters, what then! Remember the tree struck by lightning near the dockyard? It may have been just such a sudden storm that caused that,' he reminded her.

Then he told the others about a great storm the captain had once told him about, when he'd been on the ship, and everyone listened. Amu always had such interesting stories!

Finally, they decided to go to sleep, crossing the main long passage and finding another longer room, bigger than the one they'd slept in the previous night. That one was full now; the signs of storm had brought more folk inside. The girls slept on one side and the boys on the other; the centre of the room was like a passage, and anyone could move down along side without waking up the others.

Very soon, they were all asleep. Only Xerxes lay awake for a while, thinking about the riddle of the map and how they were going to deal with the ruthless men who were set on getting their hands on it. Soon, he too was asleep.

Throughout the huge storm, they didn't stir; only Joker cocked his ears two hours later, hearing the rustle of a figure moving around outside. He sniffed; it was a scent he had picked up earlier today, and one he decidedly didn't like.

It was nearing dawn, and the sky had lightened; but the figure slunk away without seeing him. Very good luck, as the figure was none other than Uri, who had been looking for the children everywhere.

None of them were any wiser about the narrow escape they'd just had!

What Xerxes overhears!

Sleeping soundly, the five children woke up late next morning, to the sound of noisy chatter. Hurriedly, they made neat little bundles of their shawls and sundry articles and set off to the riverside for a refreshing bath. The sunlight danced on the small ripples of water. After the storm of the previous night, everything was bright, freshly washed, as Kaveri observed, delighted.

On this lovely, brave new day, the children felt better; ready to face anything it might bring. They hoped desperately that Kartik's father would arrive soon. 'We can't just keep waiting, it's been two days. Why, oh why, doesn't Appa come?' asked Kaveri, for the hundredth time, her face woeful. Namami reassured her often, saying there definitely had to be a good reason for the delay.

They found berries on some thorny bushes, and sweet papayas and bananas; the perfect breakfast. Most of the fallen leaves were soggy with the night's storm, but Joker had found some dry leaves, and as they blew around in the fresh morning breeze, he chased them as though they were live rats! Kaveri giggled and said as much.

Amu Darya told them how cats were sacred in Egypt, and that if anyone killed a cat, he was put into prison, and then there was a death penalty! This sounded so strange to the children; they hadn't even heard of things like death penalty before.

'I suppose cats are important because they kill rats, who eat the harvested grain. Otherwise everyone would starve. And this way, they stop disease from spreading, rats spread disease,' reasoned Namami.

She was immediately interested, and there was a big discussion on medicine, disease, and the medical customs of other countries.

They were interrupted just then by a sight which was common for the four from Anantpur, but a novelty for Amu. A peacock came up, followed by five brown peahens. The peacock just walked ahead, then stopped suddenly and opened out its beautiful tail, full of jewel bright colours of blue and green.

How Amu stared in delight! 'I have seen so many now, after coming here, but I never tire of this sight. This area is full of peacocks I know, but we don't have them in Mesopotamia; at least I don't remember hearing of them. I wish I could describe them to everyone back home, but I will never be able to do justice to the glorious colours. My brothers and sisters would love them.'

'Amu, just take a few fallen feathers back with you. They'll get the idea,' suggested Namami.

'Hey, why didn't I think of that,' exclaimed Amu.

'Because you are a boy, and boys don't think!' shot back Namami, with a big grin.

The others roared with laughter, and then, laughter subsiding, picked up again where they had left off; the cloth map and the symbols and the mysterious bits of seal—things that were never far from their minds now. They were determined to solve the riddle of the map.

On the soft, damp sand, they drew a large, accurate picture of the map using the copy Kartik had made.

They sat and puzzled and puzzled over it. Amu came up with some good ideas. Having been on a boat, he had seen navigation maps and was familiar with the usage of symbols.

'They have shown us that we need to look in a place where there are hills, and boats,' he said.

'Which could be anywhere! Why the sun and moon here though?' wondered Namami.

'Directions?' they pondered. 'South, west, east or north?'

'Wish they had put in the pole star… we would have known the north then,' said Amu Darya.

'If only all the pieces of the seal were there, we'd have some idea,' repeated Kartik, for the hundredth time. 'I know it's a link, I can feel it.'

He had an idea. 'Hey, folks, let's ask an artisan if they know what this is. I'll find one of the people from yesterday.' He was thrilled with himself, and the others, on hearing his plan, agreed it was a great idea. It was time to get moving, and they rose eagerly.

Kaveri and Namami had been busy with their fingers in the meanwhile, as everyone else brainstormed. They had collected thin reeds and were busy weaving small baskets and punnets to take to the markets. All girls were very good at this, and wove reeds, long grass, and long leaves from the maize and corn plants into household containers. Namami's parents constantly needed these, and in their home no one's hands were ever idle!

'That's a very fine collection you've made today,' marvelled Amu, who was used to see reeds being woven in Mesopotamia. Of course Kartik and Xerxes took no notice, as they were also used to this constant weaving. They helped carry the baskets, and together the five set off.

'You people carry on to the lower town as you had planned, I am going to the dockyard,' announced Xerxes. 'I want to check with a sailor about the map's indication of a place with hills and boats. And alone, this time, there are too many people who may recognize Joker and one of the girls. Kartik and Amu are with you, Kavi, so you will be safe,' he added. The previous day's stories of sunsets and moonlit nights and purple seas had set his imagination afire. He would go and meet some sailors while he was investigating!

Keeping a watchful eye out for their foes, the children set off. They went off to the lower town to meet potters and fishermen and artisans.

Namami had her new clothes on and had kept her new hairstyle, of which she was very proud. She looked like a young lady now, not a girl.

Kartik walked quickly, longing to see the workshops, to view the furnaces where the seals were baked, how they were carved, and the drawings and painting on the pottery. He was determined to find just what that seal was.

Xerxes, in the meanwhile, was already in his element. He stood still at the dockyard, observing the activity all around him. Two small boats had docked, and there were sailors disembarking; wheelturners who knew everything about the tides, winds, and the different routes to take at different times: during the monsoons, storms, or in placid weather. They knew all the routes to the ports of the Fertile Crescent and other far off lands.

It was a totally different world. There was no talk of fields, floods, water storage, cattle and oxen, wells and irrigation, earthquakes—the topics Xerxes had heard discussed all his life. Here the talk was of the lock for the gates to close at high tide and the height of the waves, the sea and nautical conditions. 'Now this is more like it!' he thought, listening enthusiastically.

He watched a bandy-legged sailor laughing and talking; he could now make out who the sailors were because of their peculiar, rolling gait, something Amu Darya had pointed out to him. Then, his gaze fixed on two people who were talking intently but were constantly looking over their shoulder or sideways. Something about the stance of the taller man caught his attention. 'Those men! They are the same people who were with us on the elephant.'

Xerxes hid behind a pile of goods quietly, bent on finding out more about the robbery. What exactly had been so important about the contents of that bag, about its connection to the robbery, that they would kidnap Namami?

He listened intently. But this was so disappointing; they were talking of ordinary things like food and oxen and boats and cargo. After five minutes, Xerxes changed his position: he was feeling cramped, and pretended he was searching for something, in case anyone noticed him. He managed to creep right around, closer now; if he put his arm out he could touch them. The words were definitely clearer now.

He heard them say 'Ah, Sohrab… ' and then missed a few words.

'We were so late because of that wretched child yesterday. Now we have to meet him in the town near the home of the chief merchant… the public garden there… There are so many people there, no one will notice us.'

The minute Xerxes heard the name 'Sohrab', his ears pricked up. Could it be the man they had met yesterday? He'd also said he was late. The sun was much lower in the sky, was how he had put it.

Excited, Xerxes decided at once, 'I'll follow those men. And now I know how to get there... I'll just race across using the shortcut and wait at the beginning of the noblemens' road. All their houses are on the same road, the broad one, with trees and a lovely breeze. The chief merchant surely has his house there.'

He sped ahead, wondering all the while if he had the time to go and tell the others as well.

'I'll listen first, and then go. After going to the shellcutters and the furnace room, they are coming to the market. They'll be hungry.' They'd all been eating fruit and berries, which grew abundantly, but they would want a more substantial meal now.

As Xerxes ran swiftly, his mind was racing: what would he find out? Would it be about the robbery? Would he figure out the meaning of the drawing on the cloth? Hills—finger pointing rock—water—boats. It was truly a riddle.

The meeting

Xerxes reached the garden he'd heard the men speaking of, quickly, making use of the knowledge he'd acquired of local shortcuts. It was a very beautiful garden, flowering with orange fire-flowers, small bushes, abundantly covered with purple and white blooms, and fragrant greenery. Logs of wood were placed around it as benches, and shady trees and shrubs made the place an oasis of calm. Only a few people walked about, passing through. Xerxes hid behind a thick bush near the entrance; this way he could silently trail the men after they entered and hear them talk.

He was just in time! A few minutes later, the men he'd overheard came into view. They were speaking in the local language, Mehluhhi, so Xerxes could understand them perfectly.

As they passed him, one of them said, 'Sohrab will come soon and we'll get the other half of the map from him, Uri.'

'Ah!' Uri exclaimed, his eyes glittering with greed, 'Hammur! What riches we'll have! Land, fields, slaves!'

'But first, Uri, we have to find the stolen figures and jewels, and carry them to Mesopotamia,' replied Hammur.

'So they are the thieves, or at least their friends. And the map will lead them to the stolen treasures.' Xerxes noted with both satisfaction and apprehension.

He felt his ears must be like an elephant's, grown tenfold with the effort of trying to listen! He was straining so hard to hear every word and it just wasn't possible as the two men were walking ahead; he realized he'd have to follow them.

They were out of earshot now. Xerxes was disappointed and dismayed. Stealthily looking around, he heard footsteps. 'I'll have to find another place to hide. I wonder if I should just climb up this jackfruit tree? I won't be visible, it'll be perfect! But no, I'll attract attention now, if I move from here,' he thought. 'If they walk further away, I'll just creep up near them when I feel they won't notice, it's a chance I'll have to take.'

He heard footsteps again, then: the sound of footwear, short, soft: tap, tap, tap (chuk-k thap-thap). The steps stopped near his hedge. He peered through the leaves; the footsteps belonged to none other than Sohrab, of the day before, just as he'd guessed!

The tall fair man, with his long beard and scar prominent on his forehead, approached the bush that was Xerxes' hiding place and stood with his back to him; the men heard him and they turned around and walked hastily towards him.

They moved a few steps away, and this was wonderful for Xerxes, as he could watch them, unnoticed, yet hear them!

'Peace be with you,' Sohrab said to them, palms upturned.

'And with you too,' both replied, also with their palms upturned. Polite greetings done with, the men introduced themselves.

'Debu sent you, didn't he? He described you well,' added Uri, 'I hope you are satisfied with your shelter.'

The stranger nodded his head courteousely, indicating that he was.

The three sat on the ground, under the restful shade of a large jackfruit tree with its dark green leaves. How Xerxes wished he could sneak up its branches and vanish into its greenery. Red-vented bulbuls were chattering away in its branches, and it looked so peaceful and safe.

He listened intently. The polite conversation continued of course, as no one ever came to the point at once; it was considered impolite to talk business immediately on meeting.

At last came the question which he was waiting for: 'Sohrab, I believe you have brought something for us.'

'I have,' agreed Sohrab. 'But I can give it to you only after you give me a certain parcel. Those were my instructions, and I have to honour them.'

'Unfortunately Sohrab, we have lost that packet, but we are sure to find it soon... Meanwhile, please could you kindly hand over the parcel to us? We would be so very grateful to you. We know the names of the people who gave it to you: Kadir, Debu. It is really safe to give it to us.' Hammur and Uri were trying to sound as convincing as they could, hoping Sohrab would unquestioningly accept what they said. But to Xerxes' sharp ears, their sugary tones were over anxious to please Sohrab.

'Sorry.' The stranger was very polite, but equally firm. 'I have been told to exchange it with your packet... I cannot just give it to you.'

Xerxes watched with bated breath. So this is why Hammur and Uri were so desperate to have the missing parcel. The men continued cajoling and arguing by turn, but Sohrab was adamant: no parcel from them, no parcel from him. He was going to stick to what he had been told to do.

Xerxes wondered if the two would harm Sohrab; both Hammur and Uri looked irritated and angry. There seemed to be no solution at hand.

Then Xerxes heard Sohrab say, 'I'll wait for the parcel, you try and find it. We'll meet near the dockyard after an hour. 'Farewell,' he said, rising and nodding his head, and finally bowing and beginning to walk away. He appeared a purposeful man who was very clear about what his duty was, to those who had sent him.

'Wait! We'll meet you after lunch... here in the citadel. There is a merchant's house, burnt and charred looking. Come there, and we'll have it for you,' shouted Uri.

The tall man raised his hand to agree and made a dignified gesture of farewell, then walked off. Uri and Hammur began to squabble at once, blaming each other. 'I thought if we gave the names of Debu, and Kadir, he would hand it over,' snapped Hammur. Their acrimonious exchange continued.

'We could do the drawing again. I have it in my mind quite clearly... but what about that heavy, dull looking object that was in the bag? Why did we have to carry it?' asked Uri, sounding puzzled.

'I'm tired of all this. What appeared so simple has become a real problem, all because of that bag exchange. Let's look for that stupid child again. How she managed to escape is beyond me—and we couldn't spot her anywhere. We even visited the lower town this morning,' flared up Hammur, looking surly.

Xerxes stayed absolutely still in his hiding place though he was thrilled inside, never having imagined he would witness such drama.

'We have to capture that Sohrab and take the packet from him.' growled Uri, in response. He was angry at losing what he had expected to get at once, his vision of an idle, lazy life full of luxury was receding a little.

Hammur scowled in obvious irritation. 'How will you manage? He looks so strong!'

'I know! Why don't we give him a false package?'exclaimed Uri, as the idea grew in his evil mind.

'But surely he will check and then come looking for us?' objected Hammur, his look saying that he thought this was a foolish idea.

'We can make sure he doesn't. Lets work it out, Hammur. I am sure we can come up with something.' Said Uri.

'That is the most sensible idea I have heard from you in a long time, Uri,' said Hammur, with what, Xerxes was sure, was a cunning smile.

The men got up and walked away, out of the garden. Xerxes knew they were out to find little Kaveri and Namami. 'They'll do anything to get the truth out of them. They will use violence, see what they did to Nami, the unscrupulous people! I must run and tell the girls to stay hidden,' he told himself.

Making sure the men were nowhere in sight, he once again cautiously took the short cut. Charging off, his mind raced as he went over everything they would have to do to foil the plans of sinister Uri and Hammur. First, Joker had to be left with someone else for at least two hours, so the thieves wouldn't spot the girls; he was sure they could ask someone in the marketplace to keep him safely tied up. Next, he and the other boys had to follow Uri and Hammur to their second, possibly violent, meeting with Sohrab to thwart them.

Made breathless by the speed of his flight, Xerxes reached the marketplace, but search as he might, there was no sign of the girls, or Kartik or Amu.

Maybe they were still in the lower town—probably the best place to hide as the thieves had already been there. He'd heard them say so. Stopping just long enough to have a long drink of water from the cool stream nearby, he sprinted to the lower town. He had to stop and sit down once though; he had a stitch in his side, from running so soon after drinking water!

Starting up again in a few minutes, he arrived at the potters' kilns, bursting with the news he carried: news of impending danger and a villainous plot to capture an innocent man.

The lower town and the artisans

In the meanwhile, the other four were enjoying themselves in the lower town, having chatted happily with fishermen, who were mending their nets by the river and the potters by the kilns, and anyone they could find outside the workrooms.

Here were craftsmen, painters, glazers who were taking a small break from their wonderful, intensive work. There was a huge pile of clay bricks lying outside; these were the bricks with which all the houses were built.

Kaveri remarked, as a pile of teak logs caught her eye, thinking of Xerxes, 'So they build ships as well!' Boats were being made here; logs were floated down the river and collected for boat building. This was an industry in itself; many countries got their ships from Lothal, as they didn't have as much wood themselves, to build boats.

On seeing an artisan, all four gave the traditional greeting, and Namami asked, very respectfully and politely, 'Please may we see everything? We will be very careful.'

The serious looking man nodded, saying they could go to any of the workshops, but had to be careful near the furnace rooms.

As they walked towards the workshops, a woman called out to them, saying, 'Oh, this dog, is he yours? Two men had come looking for this dog, black and white, and two girls. They have left, but they seemed very anxious to meet you. They are your father's friends, I believe.'

The children looked at each other knowingly. They knew who these men were! Uri and Hammur, for sure. Whew! So now they were safe, at least for a while.

'Thank you for telling us,' Kaveri smiled at the lady and the four continued walking. Joker had in the meanwhile gone up to her in his friendly manner, of course, wagging his tail and giving her a wide, idiotic grin, cocking one ear up and then letting the other droop! How they had laughed with relief: Namami was safe for the time being, no one would come after them a second time, and so very soon.

Then, they walked to see the shell-cutters, who were sitting, making bangles and ladles, eyes narrowed and intense concentration showing on their creased brows. 'It's so amazing, actually seeing this… something I had only imagined,' said Kartik, bearing in mind that the men could still reappear.

Kaveri was gifted many shell bangles; she jingled her hands in pleasure! She was also given a necklace which she proudly and promptly wore. Their village lay near a river, but these particular shells were only found in these shallow waters around the Kathiawad and Kutch regions. Being difficult to come by, the Anantpur children didn't have any shell bangles.

'How generous and nice these artisans are!' said Kaveri, looking at her beautiful gifts. Namami soon found herself engrossed in talking to two women dressed in bright ochre and red garments, which had bold borders at the hem.

'Lo-ok, you people, I've seen the beautiful red pottery ware, I've seen the designs of antlers of the black deer looking over their heads; now just hurry up.' Amu laughed, and gently took the girls away from the artisans' wares. Kartik, of course, could have daydreamed in his artist's paradise for much longer!

The group left the workshop and went outside, Namami thanking the artisans as she left, telling them how much she appreciated their generosity: 'Thank you for these two cups and one ladle, I know my mother will really appreciate them.' Outside, someone tugged on her skirt, and when she turned around there were two little girls, squealing with laughter. As she chatted with them, the sunlight picked out the patterns on their skirts and made them appear even brighter.

Kartik, in the meanwhile, moved to a separate room, a special one, which had a furnace for heating metal. Here, a section was used for the making of moulds, and for melting bronze. The younger artist explained how it worked. It was a special technique.

A clay figure was made, coated with wax; next, another clay outer layer was made with holes, and molten bronze was poured through these holes so the wax dissolved and evaporated, letting the liquid metal harden and the bronze figure remain. The outer clay coating was then chipped away. Kartik was absolutely enthralled, for he realized he was seeing something very rare. No one from Anantpur knew this technique.

So this is how the famous dancing girl statue was created! Here, there were three other bronze dancing girls, each one with an arm through the other's. What beauty! What concentration these artists showed. He didn't dare interrupt, even to ask questions that were tumbling around in his head: 'What vision do these artists have, which they feel they have to express in their art? How sacred is their work?' These were just some of them. He decided to save this for later.

The girls wandered up and joined Kartik and they all walked outside to another workshop where men worked on stone. Kartik held his breath as he saw one artist skilfully etching on a seal a figure seated, with animals around him, practically Pashupati, the lord of animals!

Something clicked in his brain... but he wasn't going to say anything now. 'Maybe, just maybe, this was the important missing clue!' he thought, exultantly. He quietly went over to one of the carvers to ask if he could help identify the bits of seal he had with him.

Just then Xerxes came running up, panting and short of breath.

The four looked at him and saw he was big with news. Murmuring a quick thank you, they surrounded Xerxes, agog with interest.

'I've got something very important to tell you. Let's find a quiet place near the water.' The others were bursting with curiosity, but had to keep a tight rein on their patience, till they found a secluded spot.

The five found a shady spot, and sat down on an upturned old boat, wondering what could be so pressing. 'Now, Xerxes tell us!' said Amu impatiently.

'First, Those men are looking for you, Kavi and Nami, but they have come here earlier.'

'Oh, we know that,' said Namami easily. 'A lady told us as soon as we came, so we aren't scared anymore. And what wonderful things we have seen… '

'Forget that, and listen to me,' ordered Xerxes.

Then he told them about Hammur and Uri, the meeting, and their evil plans for Sohrab.

'So you see, we have to go and do something to help Sohrab,' he concluded.

They talked over all they had heard and decided what had to be done.

The bundles were to be given to Namami, so even if the men saw the boys, they would not be able to get their hands on the package.

They decided to break for a snack, as the women had hospitably plied them with some food, knowing that children were always hungry! As they ate, they continued speculating on the mystery, and why the object they had hidden in the well could be so important.

'So that Sohrab didn't give them his packet... What will they do now?' exclaimed Namami. She remembered the dark passage that had been her only escape, with a little lurch in her stomach.

Everyone was sure that the packet held clues that would complete the map, and give directions to the place where the stolen temple treasure was kept.

'All those gold figures... and how much jewellery, we have no idea!' muttered Kartik, as he puzzled the pieces together and remembered the news of the great robbery.

'Where did you run off, Kartik?' asked Kaveri inquisitively.

Still pondering about the seal, Kartik had wandered back to the artisans in the worshops. He told the group something exciting; he had made a discovery when he'd shown the artisans the broken bits of seal. 'I asked an artistisan what the bits were, and he didn't know. But he took me to an old artist, who just squinted at the pieces, and uttered one word: Pashupati, which means lord of the animals.'

'He recognized it, and one of the younger people there said he has seen one full seal somewhere, he will find it and give it to us,' said Kartik, triumphantly.

Just then, the young boy who was apprenticed to the senior artisan came running up to them. 'My guru told me about this special seal, just now. You can't see the animals, because it is part of a bigger seal. It has the Pashupati, surrounded by animals, sitting under a peepul tree. There are only three big tablets...we are not allowed to make more without the priest-king's permission. They are the only ones square in shape. The others are rectangular. These are used for very special religious occasions only.

'Where did you get these pieces?' he asked eagerly. He had to go back and report to his guru. Amu hastily told the boy that they didn't know, as it was with them by mistake.

'Wow, we're getting closer and closer,' exclaimed Namami.

Kartik bent down and drew the map he had in his mind on the sand, with a sharp rock, where the boy had drawn the original seal of the Pashupati with the animals, sitting under a tree, to show them how it looked.

All five children crowded round it. 'Wish I knew the significance of the bits of seal,' muttered Xerxes.

'It has to mean something important, otherwise it wouldn't be with the scroll,' agreed Amu, seeing no answer in sight.

But Kartik had just got a brainwave, and he shouted for their attention, his eyes bright with a new idea. 'Maybe the treasure is buried under the tree,' he whispered in a hushed tone, looking around to see if anyone could overhear.

'It is a peepul tree, the Pashupati always sits under a peepul tree. All we have to do is find this peepul tree.' His voice trailed off, as he realized the impossibility of the task at hand.

There were peepul trees all over, and many had yogis sitting underneath, meditating or praying, as it was considered a holy tree.

'How will we know which one?' asked little Kaveri. Everyone pondered over this one. How, how, how, were they to know?

They tried to make a few guesses. 'Let's just sit here for a few minutes more, before we go anywhere, it's so pretty here near the stream, we may be able to hit on some kind of solution,' begged Namami, finally, longing for some peace in the middle of all this chaos. They watched black snake-birds putting their heads in the stream, looking for fish, so only their curved snake-like necks could be seen.

Then, they made plans. The girls would remain here as they wanted to spend more time with the artisans. They would then head to the marketplace where they would be safe in the crowd. The boys would go to the burnt house and then they would all meet at the marketplace in two hours. Little did they realize that things could, and would go horribly wrong!

'Make sure that Joker is not with you when you come, though,' warned Xerxes.

'We'll ask that friendly lady to tie him up, when we leave this place,' decided Namami.

More plans were made, and the boys grew wildly excited—and scared as well—to think they would help Sohrab.

Only Amu seemed suddenly quiet, and had a distracted look on his face. The others knew at once what he was thinking about—his father, of course.

'That scroll, Amu, I think you are right, it is a map... all those pictures of various things,' said Xerxes, trying to distract him and bringing his attention again to the matter at hand. Surprisingly, his stammer seemed to have vanished.

Kaveri exclaimed, 'We're so close... I just know we're going to find out what this all means!'

'We'll definitely find the burnt-looking house. Thank goodness these people are so good hearted. The girls will be very safe here,' announced Kartik.

And maybe, just maybe, they might solve this mystery, he thought!

The white parrot

The boys sat on a large rock, as they discussed their plan of action.

'We should go to the burnt house early and hide ourselves,' suggested Xerxes with a thoughtful look.

'It was a good idea of yours, Kartik, to give the bundles and bits of seal to the girls. Even if they see us, we won't have the bundles, that should bother them and make them wonder if we really do have them.'

'And remember Nami's face when we told her to carry them. She didn't have any answer to our good reasons. Normally she'd have told us to carry them ourselves,' he added with a chuckle.

Just then they saw a pure white parrot fly past them, and then return, perching itself on a branch.

Yes a white parrot! Ite was so white that if you were to put it near snow, the snow would look grey!

It had the palest rainbow feathers trailing a little from its back—a tinge of pink, a flash of silver and blue. It looked like a white waterfall, with rainbow glints.

Amu looked at the parrot and was overjoyed. 'This is considered very lucky in Mesopotamia,' he cried, delighted. 'I'll spend this time making more enquiries about my father. This is a sign for me to continue my search. My wish is going to be granted. I can feel he's close-by. Today I will find him, I feel sure of it. Maybe the boat people will be able to tell me something, I will go to them now,' he said in sudden excitement. So saying, he fell on his knees and called on all the Gods of his land.

An, oh, God of the sky, hear me!
Enlil, God of the wind
Utu, God of sun
Enki, God of water
Nannar, God of Moon
Hear me and help me

Listen to the prayers of your humble servant. I have been created on earth to serve you, and all gods, and I have tried to do so to the best of my ability.

You have sent out a sign that you have a special blessing for me.

Help me, help me, help me!

Hope shone bright and beautiful on his face. Xerxes and Kartik looked on, deeply moved by his entreaties. They too, prayed to the spirits of the air, earth, water, sun, and sky to aid Amu

Darya, as he tried to find his father, and to help them in their quest.

There was something special about this day, thought Xerxes. He had a feeling that everything was going to happen all at once.

'We will stay with you, Amu,' said Xerxes in a decided tone.

'Yes, after all, we are your friends, we'll also go around and ask various people,' added Kartik.

They headed to the marketplace and seperated, Amu's heart full of hope and fear, and great anticipation. Surely he would get news of his father today, he thought, almost running along, a spring in his step. In his entire stay in this land, he had never before seen a white parrot. A white parrot! The special sign of his gods, the white colour standing as a powerful symbol of a wish being granted. The gods wouldn't be so unkind as to send him a sign, fill him with hope and then abandon him!

Amu thought of the joy his family would feel when he took his father home.

He looked around for the boat people. He was sure they would have news of his father. Their camp had to be somewhere around here. The boat people never stayed in any built-up shelter like the rooms near the granary; they chose to live in the open instead. Maybe they were in the maidan, or the lower field?

On his way out of the marketplace, to the maidan, he passed some familiar faces, but in his present state could barely stop to exchange polite greetings with them. He passed the rishi who was always without clothes, exposed to the elements and so deep in his meditation that sun, rain, wind, and cold, all made no difference to him. Standing on one leg—bearded, hair coiled on his head, hands by his side—he made a magnificent figure in his yogic concentration. The first time Amu had seen this posture, his eyes had been riveted to the yogi; in his country there were no yogis. He was used to him now, and carried on past him and all the people gathered together in little groups, laughing at the sight of monkeys grabbing fruit from a man, en route.

At last, he spotted, the boat people. Dressed differently from other groups, they at once stood out in this gathering of different clans and tribes. Quietly, Amu approached a serious-faced man who was wearing long rudraksha beads, his torso bare except for a long white cloth flung over one shoulder.

The man didn't put out his hands or open his palms the way Amu did; he had a different greeting. Solemnly, he folded his hands together in front of his chest and bowed his head, his response to Amu's greeting. 'And what can I do for you, son?' he asked in a deep voice, with a sing song accent. It was almost as though he was singing rather than talking! Some of the words were familiar, similar to Meluhhi, while many were different; but their meaning was clear to Amu.

Knowing that the Meluhhi he spoke would not make any sense, at least not much to this man from eastern parts, from Gangaland (he remembered being told when they had seen the caravan of boats come in the previous night), he looked around appealingly, desperate for help, desperate and silent. Where had Kartik and Xerxes gone to? He couldn't see them anywhere. After many months, he suddenly felt like a foreigner again.

Then his eyes fell on a monkey. Not just any monkey, but Binku, Shyon's monkey. Sure enough, there was Shyon waving out to him. The boy bounded up and greeted Amu. Amu was relieved to see his cheerful face, and asked him for help at once.

'Shyon, please tell them I am looking for a sailor or trader from a far off land. Or ask if any newcomer has recently joined their tribe? In the last two years?'

The man shook his head in reply to Shyon's question. He smiled at both. Then he pointed to another group of people. Amu managed to say, 'Peace be with you,' before sprinting away, taking Shyon with him.

This group was made up of five men, all much older than his father. Shyon asked them the same question, and Amu looked hopefully at the group, only to see heads being shaken in a definite no. He continued on like this for a while.

Finally, he walked away slowly and sat down, heavily. He put his head on his knees and didn't look up. What was the use of all the signs, he wondered. His was an impossible mission. And he'd have to go back and admit defeat; then his mother's heart would break. He had failed. He wouldn't be taking his father back to his own land.

Sunk in despair, he didn't look up even when he felt a light touch on his shoulder. Then, feeling a tug at his shoulder, he glanced up, eyes bright with unshed tears.

It was Shyon again, gentle Shyon, with Binku on his shoulder, who he had almost forgotten in his own private grief. 'Tell me brother, what troubles you? I will try to help.'

Amu Darya simply shook his head, overwhelmed by a deep feeling of loss, his disappointment almost filling the air. He pulled himself together, squared his shoulders and took a great big gulp.

'Today isn't over,' he said bravely. Then very simply, in a few words, he told his story yet again.

Struck by Amu's story, just as everyone else was, Shyon felt as sad as the four children had felt. 'I'll help. And I do believe in omens. Your white parrot means something, my friend. The day hasn't ended, the sun has yet to sink, so keep hope alive in your heart, my friend. I must return to my people as we are off to the riverside to offer prayers, but I will be back soon!' Reassuring Amu, he sprang up and away, running after Binku, who was already busy harassing a young boy.

The priest-king's prophecy

Amu sat up, alone again, and decided to put all of this behind him. After all, for two months he had been facing this disappointment, in every new place he had visited. He thought of the different places he had been to: Ranginapur, Dwarka, Mayurpur, Bhuj, Tapiti, Narmanadi; by river boat, on foot, on the back of any animal that was at hand, in ox-carts. He was overwhelmed by the difficulty of this task he had undertaken. He felt subdued and almost defeated by its enormity. And alongside this, the mystery of the missing treasure of Mohenjo-daro. So much seemed to be happening to him, all at once!

A small muffled sound escaped him, and he sat down hastily, pretending to look down, shaken by small sobs, a small, lost, defenceless figure.

He suddenly felt a hand on his back, this time a gentle hand... a large hand. He lifted his head and stood up at once when he saw the man who had touched him so gently, so commanding was his presence. For he was of stately bearing, with a tidy beard and neatly combed hair which was held in place with a shining, deeply etched golden metal band. An imposing ornament hung heavily over and below his ears, and he wore a finely woven, richly embroidered shawl with a flowered trefoil border, draped over his shoulder. With it, he wore a pure white veshti made of the softest cotton.

Amu recognized him at once as one of three great priest-kings of Mohenjo-daro. He was here only to lead the prayers on the auspicious start of the Surya Mela. The three priest-kings were the masters of religion, wise and loved by all, and they were on the governing councils of the tribes and clans, which they looked after. All three were from different regions. People obeyed these men, and took their problems and grievances to them. They helped to keep law and order, so everyone lived in peace and harmony.

'Sir... sir... sir,' Amu stammered, almost speechless before this man who seemed to have such an air of compassion, power, and dignity.

'My child, what ails you? Perhaps I can help, for I see deep sorrow written in your young eyes,' the priest-king said in a gentle tone.

Amu Darya couldn't keep himself from responding honestly. There was such authority about this man, it made his question seem like a command! Out poured the whole tragic story of Amu's missing father.

'And he always said, 'You are Amu Darya, my life water, my Amu,' he ended, brokenly.

The priest-king patted him on his back tenderly and strangely Amu felt a little better, with that one simple gesture.

'Such a big burden, such a great mission, for so young a person… and such great courage as you have shown! I can help you, for this is where grown-ups can help—I know many people from far and wide, who have travelled from great distances for this Surya Mela. I shall send the word around. Fear not, now your mission is my mission, I will help you.'

He stated this last bit with confidence and certainty. Amu felt as though a great weight had been lifted from his shoulders. He looked up at the priest-king with total faith and acceptance in his eyes. Though he was from a different land, and was young, his heart told him that in this great, serene man, was a purity of soul not to be doubted. He no longer felt dejected.

'O Priest of all temples, I will carry on, but now I feel I have a grown-up to whom I can turn, so my task feels easier and my heart is light. I beg leave of you.' Amu bowed low. Though some of the words were not quite right, he uttered them with a deep dignity.

The priest-king put out his hands, palms open, and murmured, 'May all you look for be achieved. Peace be with you.' His voice was tranquil now. And somehow, despite the odds, Amu again felt hopeful.

He leapt up, and started walking, looking out for the other two. He must certainly try and find the treasure that this great man wanted returned to the temple. He now felt this was of utmost importance, it had a much greater urgency than before. Somehow the white parrot, the priest-king, the treasure, his father, all seemed linked.

'Amu, Amu!' he heard his name being called. Xerxes and Kartik had returned.

Kartik's face looked sad.

'Oh, Amu, we asked around. No one seems to have heard of him. Nor has Appa come,' he told him.

All three continued talking, as Amu told them of the priest-king's prophecy. It was getting late now, time to go for the meeting at the burnt house.

Treachery

'All three went by the short cut to the raised town, and to the clean, broad streets where the merchants had their dwellings.

'We need to find a good hiding place' said Kartik.

Amu said, 'Oh, there are a few trees, so it will be easy.'

They crossed a couple of streets and came to the burnt house. It was a two-storeyed blackened mansion, surrounded by a wall. There was a large courtyard with a well. It had the dead, vacant look of an abandoned house, desolate and sad. Its bricks were black and grey with ash from the fire; it had even scorched the top storey of the house!

'Just the place to meet someone and rob him' thought Kartik, with a shiver. The place was so silent and eerie.

Amu and Xerxes looked around. Kartik saw a mango tree and another, tall, leafy tree, which would hide one of them very well. But whoever climbed that would have to climb higher! Amu, the most agile of the boys, quickly decided he would hide there. He swiftly climbed so high that he was totally invisible.

Kartik and Xerxes climbed onto the sturdy mango tree; Xerxes had learnt from his last spying mission on Hammur and Uri that a tree was the best spot to watch and listen from. There were many branches up there to hide them completely. They had enough time to find a good hiding place, with thick, strong branches to take their weight, and close enough to whisper to one another. And so, they lay in wait.

The tree had started to blossom, they noticed. 'We'll have mangoes early this year, Xerxes,' whispered Kartik, smelling that wonderful green-mango smell of the flowers. They could hear a koel hidden in the leafy greenery of the tree, calling, 'Kuhoo, ku-oo, ku-oo kuhoooo.'

Time passed slowly. 'Hey look, see those red eyes? It's the female koel, she is so black, just like a crow.' They waited, yawning and shifting clumsily, growing impatient. It wasn't all that comfortable after a while, though it was cool and breezy and they felt safe, well hidden from view.

Bored and fed up, they decided the men weren't coming and started to climb down the tree, yawning. 'It's so foolish to keep waiting,' muttered Kartik, who was feeling cramped. But just as they had begun their descent, they heard a cough. Quick as lightning and as silently as possible, they were back in their places. They heard footsteps. Someone was approaching: they were Uri and

Hammur, looking crafty and smug at the thought of their secret plan.

Kartik clutched Xerxes' arm, realizing now that this was real. They had a treasure to recover, and they had to foil the plans of two angry, probably violent men. Quietly, Xerxes pressed Kartik's arm hard, warningly, with one finger pressed to his lips as if saying, 'No talking now!' Kartik thought of the time when he had knocked out that boar, that seemed like years ago, and how lucky he had been. That same luck might not help them now, he thought.

A few minutes later, Sohrab appeared. They heard Uri (Xerxes knew it was him from his slightly nasal voice) greet Sohrab, and Hammur say with a big laugh, 'How fortunate we were that you were kind enough to wait! Here is the package, we found it easily, it was left behind in my sleeping mat. I hadn't thought of looking there.'

A bulky package was handed over, and Sohrab took out a neatly tied, tiny package of his own.

'Here it is, my friends. And thank you for honouring my request. You see, I have to hand this,' he pointed to the packet just given to him, 'to someone else, in return for a great kindness he did for me.' He prepared to leave. 'Many thanks and may peace be with you.'

Xerxes and Kartik were following all this intently, though they couldn't see clearly as the men were now moving out of their sight. They missed the sudden action that followed!

Sohrab was walking away, without the backward glance that might have saved him—when suddenly he was struck from behind by a hard blow. He was sent flying to the ground, and as he rolled over, for good measure, Hammur gave him a sharp kick on his shinbone. Then his arms were pulled, roughly, behind him.

Uri muttered loudly and fiercely in his ears, 'You be quiet—there is no one to hear you now. Listen to what we say and maybe no harm will come to you.'

Hammur pushed a rag into a shocked Sohrab's mouth, kicked him hard again and gagged him. The men had his hands tied in a second—so well prepared were they—with rope and thick cords and a stick, all kept handy.

Meanwhile, Kartik and Xerxes had heard Sohrab's first cry of pain and then silence: quickly, they parted the leaves, looking at each other worriedly. What they saw was terribly shocking.

Near the front door of the burnt house, Uri and Hammur could be seen as they tightened the ropes which bound the now helpless Sohrab.

Amu couldn't see very well, but guessed something was up. He too tried to look through the leaves, and the same sight met his eyes.

'Lets help him!' all three thought and at once, started climbing hurriedly down the tree. Xerxes, watching poor Sohrab as he struggled, erupted violently on the scene, his eyes blazing. He picked up a big, dried up branch near him. Gentle Kartik, angered by this violence, made ready with his fists. They were the first to climb down, being much lower than Amu, who took longer to come down from his high perch. If he waited a little longer, maybe he could catch one of the men from behind, he reasoned.

The men turned around, as the boys rushed up to them, glaring and screaming. After that, there was total confusion.

Sohrab couldn't move as he was tied up, he had been so unprepared for the attack that they had overpowered him at once. Alone, he had been no match for his attackers, and now he was defenceless. He couldn't even talk, they had left him with his face on the ground.

The boys tried to grab and undo the rope, only to be struck hard by Uri. Both hit out wildly and kicked and scratched, but they were no match for the two men. Kartik was tripped up, and fell with a thud on the ground. Although Uri looked thin and slight, in reality he was wiry and had whipcord strength. He might have been pretending to be a lady on the elephant ride, but there was nothing ladylike about him now! Amu was down now, and joined in the fray.

And the dried branch that Xerxes had picked up was of no use—it broke as soon as Hammur grabbed it, when Xerxes was trying to give him a blow on the head. The boys were given a stinging slap each, and then it was their turn to be bound and tied up roughly. Amu uttered something in Sumerian and charged at the men with another short branch which he had found, and they turned to see who this third person could be.

'So, you speak Sumerian, do you? Who has sent you to spy on us? Tell us,' spat out Uri. He hadn't been hurt. He gripped Amu in a tight vice-like hold and gave him a hard, vicious shake, and raised one hand to hit him. Amu, though strong, couldn't withstand this sudden attack and fell down.

'Lets just put all of them in the house. We don't want this spy around, he may know much more than we think. We'll lock him up and question him later,' said Uri grimly, in his slightly nasal voice.

He looked at the boys who were now tied up.

'These two! These are the same boys!' yelled Hammur, excited and angry. 'They were on the elephant with us! How did they know where we were? Why are they here? We have to find out!' he added, incensed now.

'Later, later!,' shouted Uri, gnashing his teeth. He didn't want to delay leaving this place!

With a sinking heart, the boys realized that they had been too late: they'd wanted to help, but were now prisoners instead.

Quickly and efficiently, the men set about tying the boys' feet and pushed all four captives into the abandoned house. They weren't quiet either; they shouted and threatened the boys gruffly, speaking in bullying and hectoring tones. Of course, they were worse with Sohrab, sneering at the dignified man, now that he was under their control.

Sohrab was thrown into one room, solitary and alone. Kartik and Xerxes were taken up to another room on the first floor. The men lugged the boys up, hurting and bruising them badly in the bargain, and cursing the weight they had to haul upstairs.

'Now tell us quickly, what were you doing here? If you don't tell us the truth, it will be worse for you,' threatened Hammur, one arm raised in a menacing gesture.'We were playing hide and seek...' said Kartik.

'Ooh ho, so boys come to play hide and seek, do they?' sneered Uri.

'We are in a hurry now, we'll be back soon, you boys, and then just watch out!' so saying Uri, for good measure, twisted Kartik's ear till he screeched with pain.

'You better tell us the truth, if you know what is good for you... or we will make sure we take you so far away, across the seas, you will never see your family again,' he said with fury in his voice.

'We will be back shortly, so don't try any tricks,' snaped Hammur, with another swipe at Xerxes's face, which made him wince with pain.

'Let's make sure they can't yell, lets tie up their mouths.' Hammur made sure the gags were in place.

It was dark inside the room, as there was no window to let in any light.

Xerxes and Kartik were at the mercy of Hammur and Uri now! And they didn't know what those two would do to Amu!

Captive

After coming down, Uri heaved a sigh of relief. It hadn't been easy, lugging two boys up the stairs—two uncooperative boys who were a dead weight. Then, remembering Amu's earlier words, he turned to him.

'Lets just put him in the same room as that man. I cannot carry this heavy boy upstairs and it's better to separate them. We don't want this spy around, he may know much more than we think. We'll lock him up and question him later,' said Uri grimly, in his slightly nasal voice.

'Yes, a little time without food and water will make him squeal like a pig,' agreed Hammur, in a menacing tone, thinking also of the two boys upstairs. There were too many boys around today, he thought to himself. Well, they were all going to be very sorry they ever ventured into the burnt house, he would make sure of that!

He twisted Amu's arm and hissed fiercely, 'Don't try to escape. It will be worse if you do so.'

And for good measure Amu's arm was twisted just a little more, till the boy gave a cry of pain.

‘That was just the beginning. Wait and see what happens to nosy, spying boys,’ Uri declared with a snarl.

Amu was pushed into the same room as Sohrab. As a last savage touch, the two men tied his feet together and left him on the floor.

The half light threw shadows, some long, some short and unnatural, in the room. Amu was in shock. What was he doing here? This was the day he had meant to find his father. Instead, here he was, locked up with a stranger, with no rescue at hand. He started to distinguish proper shapes after the men had gone; after the bright sunlight outside, his eyes took a while to get used to the peculiar grey light in the room.

His companion, the older man, lay still, from the last hard blow Uri had given him. His face was a dim blur in the pale light of the room. But Amu could make out that he was dressed in the ordinary clothes of all the people here; a veshti and long robe-like shirt over it.

Amu's arms hurt, and he groaned. He couldn't seem to think clearly.

Most importantly, how could he, Amu, stowaway and survivor, have been stupid enough to get caught!

After all the warnings he had given Namami and Kaveri, he was the one who had been careless. Now he knew how Namami had felt, at the mercy of these men, left in the cave by these same villains. These men were cruel and dangerous. Back home in Mesopotamia they would never have dared to be so violent because they would have been punished in equal measure.

The minutes went by, silently. Then, he heard a low moan; the other prisoner, whoever he was, was regaining consciousness. He gave a muffled grunt. He rolled over and Amu, straining his eyes, saw in the half-light that the man's hands were bound like his, and that a scarf-like cloth was tied over his mouth.

Amu tried to move his hands and fingers, which were tied tightly. He knew he had to keep his fingers from getting numb; he had seen the sailors flex their fingers to do so. He felt thirsty and thought how he would have loved some water to drink.

He looked at the man again. He was stirring and trying to move about. Amu, watching him with intense concentration, realized that the scarf around his mouth was loosening; the man sensing this, was moving his face from side to side to get it off.

Amu pushed and propelled his way like a land fish towards the man, breathing hard as it was very painful even to move across this little room. He turned onto his side, his hands facing the man. Guessing what the boy wanted to do, the man lay still and turned his head so that his face was close to Amu's bound hands. Amu's fingers painfully managed to grasp the cloth and he pulled with as much strength as he could muster. At last the gag was off.

'My son, I thank you. At least I can talk and breathe easily now,' murmured the man in a hoarse, low voice.

He coughed a little. The cough reminded Amu of someone, but he couldn't remember who.

No sooner had the man spoken than the door opened and a sudden gust of wind blew in. Hammur and Uri were back, with their black looks, black hearts, and black intentions clear on their faces.

'I told you, Hammur, my hunch was right, we should never have left these two together. His hands weren't tied tight enough. We were in too much of a hurry.'

'So this is what you were up to. We were too kind to you,' yelled Uri. He pulled Amu and dragged him, screaming and shouting, to another room.

'A little isolation will be good for you, little animal that you are,' he shouted harshly, snarling at Amu. 'We'll take you away from this house,' he continued in a dangerous, low voice. 'And don't try any funny tricks.'

Meanwhile, Hammur had tied the scarf around Sohrab's mouth again and pushed him further into a corner. There was no way of escape for him now. 'Uri, we have to take this boy away from him,' he said, pointing to the man. 'But where can we go, where no one will find him… '

'I know!' exclaimed Uri, 'Should we put him in the small store room of the GRANARY?'

'Uri, you are as foolish as ever,' said Hammur irritatedly. We can't take him so far… it has to be close-by. Now let me think… '

A minute later, he gave a mean, satisfied smile.

'We'll put him in the small room at the side. It's a small bathing area, no one will go there. Now make sure he is tied so tight that he is not be able to move, or make any kind of sound.

The two men had returned to get another small axe and digging tools, which lay in the house, which was their hideout—and now the prison of four!

Appa finally arrives

Namami and Kaveri, meanwhile, spent the afternoon with the crafts people and their families, looking at their wares, finding presents to take home, all the while thinking of what Xerxes and Kartik were up to. Two hours flew by. It was time to head back to the marketplace where they said they would meet Amu and the boys. They left Joker tied up with the fisherfolk, waving goodbye to him amidst a volley of protesting barks. 'Where do you think you are going without me?' he seemed to be saying.

They planned to return to pick him up when it was safe. Their bundles were now heavier with all the small gifts they had picked up, and they had the boys' bundles as well. But they were impatient to get to the marketplace and skipped along. When they arrived, Namami laughed, saying, 'This place has become our home!'

Kaveri was busy, as usual, looking out for her father when she felt a gentle pull on her plaits. Appa always did that! She turned around and yes, at last, it was her father. She shrieked with delight, jumping up, crying out, 'Appa! Appa! What made you take so long? Where are the others? When did you come?'

There were so many questions, and she didn't give him a chance to reply before asking the next one. Her excitable dark eyes were sparkling with joy, as she hung on her father's arm and continued to ask questions.

Finally, almost breathless, she stopped talking.

'At last, Kavi, I can talk,' laughed her father with a small wink at Namami, who had greeted him in the traditional way.

'Nami, what's this grown-up dress? Have you suddenly become older?' he laughed, giving her a questioning look.

'Come sit down here and tell me what you have been up to. Where are the boys? The team has broken up, has it?' he asked, smiling at them. Spying a sheltered shady patch of grass, the three of them sat down. Appa told them about the series of mishaps that had delayed him.

'First my cart, then Akkudada's wooden shaft, then one of the bullocks refused to move. And would you believe it, my cart had another problem again! So, a series of mishaps… and of course, we had to take the road, we couldn't cut across fields like you,' he concluded with a relieved smile, looking at both the girls, who seemed well enough. 'I was so worried about you, but as you know, I am in charge, so I had to stay with them. You can imagine how anxious I was, thinking I had the responsibility of Xerxes and you, Nami!' The girls smiled, uncertain as to when they should tell Appa that actually, things had gone quite wrong.

'I was looking out for you as soon as we came, and was so anxious till Altairbhai told me he saw you daily. I was quite content after that, so we settled our things and then I came looking for you.'

'We have already lost three valuable days. Tomorrow at four in the evening the planets start their auspicious alignments so we have to be quick. Now we plan to stay for a few days after the mela gets over. My cart has to be properly fixed, no makeshift arrangements. And again—where are those boys? Where have they gone? Are they hiding from us?'

Kaveri, her eyes full of excitement and fear, lowered her voice, 'Appa we have something important to tell you,' she whispered. She knew he would be terribly upset to hear of the dangerous adventure they had got themselves caught up in.

Between her and Namami they managed, with many questions from Appa, to pour out all that had happened: the wrong bundle, the men, making friends with Amu, Namami's kidnapping.

'Nami, are you really alright? What a brave girl you are… and how did you manage to escape from that cave? Your parents will be so proud of you. Oh, why did I leave you children alone? I never thought such a thing could happen,' he lamented, picturing in his mind everything that could have gone wrong.

Kaveri and Namami continued to tell him about the map, the bits of seal, the two men, and the assignation at the old abandoned house. This was certainly a gripping tale!

'And you say the boys have gone to this burnt house to hear what Sohrab has to say?' he added, the furrows on his forehead increasing as he realized that the boys might well be in danger, at the hands of these ruthless men.

He was absolutely aghast, and wondered aloud, 'Such villains! And to think that they are connected to the great robbery! Who would have thought!'

Namami nodded her head and said in a rush, 'Those men, Appa, are not good people—see what they did to me. I am worried about the boys.' The boys should have returned by now, she realized. She felt very anxious, imagining all kinds of fearful things.

'We must go at once and find them—this is a very serious matter. We'll take strong, young Altair with us,' said Appa, confirming what the girls were both thinking. But you two girls stay here, sit right next to that lady there.' 'Don't move,' he added sternly.

'Oh, Appa, can't we come now? Altairbhai is there, and all of us... we can always run away if you tell us to,' pleaded the girls.

Reluctantly, Appa finally gave in to their pleading, mostly because he didn't want to leave the girls out of his sight again, now that he was back with them.

Appa was so full of authority and knew so clearly what to do, that they felt relieved. Namami realized only now how alone they had been all this while.

Just then a familiar, panting little creature came bounding up to them—Joker had managed to get loose and had come to find them! He jumped up and fawned at Namami, and then at Kaveri, looking the very picture of innocence!

'So this is your wonderful dog, Nami? The one who brought you back?' joked Appa.

'We left him behind as we were scared those two men, would notice us at once and do something again,' she replied. 'But he seems to have the best timing! You are here, so we are safe.'

Now that Appa was there, they had nothing to worry about, Kaveri thought, bending down to pat Joker. Though Namami scolded the little dog, she was secretly very glad; silly as it seemed to look to their new pet for support, they would need all the help they could get, against the daring robbers.

'Quick children, let's not waste any more time. We have to find the boys and stop those men,' said Appa, picking up their things.

Hastily, he swept the girls along, and went to the small granary to fetch Altairbhai, calling out his name. He was there in a second, as he had been waiting for Appa's return. Quickly Appa told him he needed help, and asked him to go along with them.

'We should look for the burnt house—and maybe we will meet them on the road, they may be returning with Sohrab,' suggested Namami, describing what the five children had pieced together earlier.

'Yes, it's in the upper town somewhere,' Kaveri chimed in. She was determined to show her father everything, including the well where they had hidden the strange map.

Altairbhai's ears pricked up, and he rubbed his chin thoughtfully. 'I think I know where this house might be,' he said.

The four of them—well four plus Joker!—took the short cut to the upper town. Talking nineteen to the dozen, Kaveri filled Altairbhai in on what had happened, Appa indulging her as he scoured the streets for a clue, a sign as to where Kartik and Xerxes might be.

Action

Altairbhai marched faster and faster up the streets, telling Appa that he was quite sure they were near the house. And then there it was—the old, blackened house, which Altair had luckily seen once before. There was an unnatural silence as they neared it; the quiet side lane seemed even quieter, the house lay sleeping in the late afternoon sunshine. Even the birds seemed more silent. Kaveri shivered.

The small group entered and immediately Appa, looking with narrowed eyes, picked up some telltale signs: flattened grass, broken twigs, leaves, a broken branch and a stick—all unusual sights in a house that wasn't being lived in.

'There has been some kind of fight here,' said Appa, raking the courtyard and garden area with a quick glance.

The four of them crept in through the courtyard, not knowing what or whom they would find. Appa made Kaveri and Namami hang back, behind Altairbhai, and even behind Joker, not knowing what to expect.

They heard a small, muffled cough, and then there was silence. Appa led them in the direction of the cough, sensing something was afoot. He spotted a door which had been blocked from the outside with boulders and bricks stacked up against it. Here was a reason to investigate! Someone had certainly made sure that whoever was inside would not be able to push it open.

Altairbhai joined him, quickly pushing the bricks aside. The door was opened in seconds.

Inside, on the floor, desperately trying to free himself, was a bound up man.

Big bruises showed on his gagged face and arms, and the scar on his forehead seemed livid. His hands and feet were tied, and the cord was tied to the bricks in the corner. There was no way he could move.

Appa gave an exclamation of anger and horror. 'What beasts did this?' he roared in fury, with pity for the helpless man who had been treated like an animal.

He and Altairbhai hurriedly, but carefully, set about freeing the poor captive, swiftly untying and cutting the cords that bound him, as they vowed to avenge this violence.

Appa and Altairbhai rubbed the man's hands and spoke gently to him. The first thing they had done was to remove the gag from his mouth. As he tried sitting, he fell over with a moan. 'My leg, my leg,' he muttered. Hammur and Uri had been cruel and had rained blows on him, hurting him badly. 'I am Sohrab, from Dholavira,' he finally managed to say, softly.

Namami had tears in her eyes and Kaveri held her hand tightly, scared to let go, though in her heart of hearts she felt safer, as Appa was in charge now.

'Get water from the well, you two,' ordered Appa. The girls ran to the doorway, for the well was at the entrance, and pulled the vessel kept for drawing water, till it came up, brimming with water. They took the vessel inside, and Sohrab took a drink of the clear water.

'Have you seen any boys... my sons?' enquired Appa, when he thought the man had recovered sufficiently enough to talk.

In the meanwhile, Altairbhai had gone upstairs, his sharp ears hearing small sounds from the floor above. One door was closed and he could hear the sound of drumming feet. It stopped as suddenly as it had started. Opening it, he exclaimed thankfully, 'Xerxes! Kartik! You are both safe. Your father is downstairs with that other man. He will be so relieved that you are fine.'

He quickly removed the gags, then started untying and cutting the ropes which bound them. The men had trussed them up like goats. It had been with great difficulty that Xerxes had raised both his tied feet at one time, and banged them down to make the noise which Altairbhai heard. He had kept doing so at intervals, hoping that someone would come and hear them. Kartik had also done the same. It seemed to be the only chance of being rescued and getting away before Uri and Hammur returned.

Both boys staggered to their feet, Kartik swaying slightly.

'They were rough, those two!' he said with a grimace.

Altairbhai took the boys down to the others. He tied the ropes around his waist: one never knew when they might come in handy, in circumstances like these, he thought.

The secret of the map

Downstairs, another drama was unfolding. Sohrab seemed to feel better. In fact, after two minutes and another drink of water later, he started getting his colour back.

'There was another boy—they have tied him up,' he said in a slightly hoarse voice. 'I have no idea where they could have put him. Has he been taken away?'

Please look for him, hurry, hurry—he helped me, he's a good lad.'

Altairbhai appeared just then, with the boys, who grinned triumphantly. There was a big commotion as everyone struggled to tell each other what had happened. When Altairbhai heard what Sohrab had said, he went to check. In a trice, they heard a shout. 'He's here!' He removed the gag with great speed, and also managed to cut the rope which bound Amu.

He pulled Amu up, saying, 'Kartik's father is here. They are with the other man.'

Both went to the room where Sohrab was, Amu hobbling, as his feet were burning and hurting badly.

He sat down, unusually quiet and looking a little dazed, while the girls fussed over him, and got water for everyone. Rubbing his burning ankles, he just listened and watched the scene in front of him, sitting with his back to the door.

Kartik was being hugged by his father, who then hugged Xerxes, saying, 'You are safe, thank all the spirits of the sun, air, sky, and water! You were in my care, I had told your father nothing would happen to you.'

Then he saw Amu, looking shaken, and gave him a gentle clap on the back and a big hug.

'You are a brave boy and a true friend,' he told the suddenly shy Amu. But praise like this from another father figure made Amu feel better!

Then Sohrab, in his hoarse voice, sounding drawn and shaken, also thanked him.

'I bless you my boy,' he murmured. Amu just nodded; he hardly seemed to be taking in anything.

Altairbhai went over to talk to Sohrab while Appa questioned the boys as to what had happened. Sohrab began to speak, when the children interrupted him, asking what he knew of Uri and Hammur's whereabouts. But Appa kept them all quiet. He wanted to hear what Sohrab had to say.

Though a little better, Sohrab still looked weak. His ordeal had left him more tired than he thought possible. He started talking, with long pauses in between.

'I knew nothing, except that I had to give them a parcel which had been sent to me by Kadir, someone to whom I owed a lot.'

'But,' and he gave his first real laugh, 'those men are in for a shock! I suspected them; there was something odd about them. So now they have the wrong parcel!'

'What?' said Appa, beginning to chuckle.

Sohrab gave a weak gust of laughter. 'Ho! Ho! How angry the men are going to be! You see, I gave them another packet as I grew suspicious of them. I somehow didn't trust them one bit. I was planning to follow them after a bit and talk to them, and then, if I trusted that they were the right people, I was going to give it to them. But they didn't give me a chance. They hit me and I knew my suspicions were correct,' he added with a frown.

How all the children cheered at this! Sohrab had thwarted the robbers yet again.

Xerxes then sat down in front of Sohrab and spoke very earnestly. 'Sir… please tell us, before you hear our whole tale, how well do you know Uri? It is very important.' Sohrab started relating the events as they took place.

'See, I was determined to come to the Surya Mela. I had my personal reasons. I had to ask the gods for something, a wish to be granted, and since the spirits of all the elements were to be invoked, I decided I had to come. We had decided to come together, Kadirbhai and I. Unfortunately, my friend Kadirbhai couldn't come, so I came alone.'

Here he swayed again, and Appa made him sit, and gave him another drink of water.

'The parcel was given by Debuda to Kadirbhai—and because of Kadirbhai's great kindness to me, I agreed to pass it on as I was coming here.'

'Kadirbhai had insisted that I only give it to Uri and Hammur. They had been described to me in detail by the messenger who carried the parcel from Kadirbhai to me. But I had to get a packet in return, I was told. The one request was that I had to be absolutely sure that I would get it and that it had to be from either Uri or Hammur. The packet was of utmost importance, under no condition was I to give mine without receiving another one in return, That was the most important part of the message. Else I was to keep my small parcel, and return it to Kadirbhai, as those were his instructions.'

Here again, Sohrab paused, took another sip of water, and then continued.

'It seemed peculiar to me, but I knew Kadirbhai must have had his own reasons, so I agreed. I saw it as my sacred duty to do exactly as I was asked.'

He looked around. There was pin drop silence for exactly ten seconds. Then what a babble of voices erupted! Xerxes quickly told Sohrab the truth: that Uri and Hammur were somehow involved in the big robbery at Mohenjo-daro, and that Sohrab had become an unknowing accomplice.

What's more, he held the key to solving the mystery of the stolen treasure's disappearance.

Sohrab was terribly shocked. To think he could have unwittingly helped steal sacred treasures! He looked even more pale and drawn than before.

'I had no idea I was carrying the other half of the map that they would use to find these stolen goods. What clever rogues those men were. I know that Kadirbhai is honest as the day and would never do anything wrong. They have used him. He has just been a pawn in a dangerous game.'

'Sohrabbhai, where have you sent the men?' Namami asked, urgently.

'Oh, I saw the map—I was told it was the location of a holy spot and very important, as buried there was a great religious item meant for the Surya Mela.

'So I drew a false map, with some hills and the dockyard and close to it I put a cross, near the tree struck by lightning. They will go and dig there.'

'That's close-by, let's go,' said Xerxes ready as always for action.

'No, we need a plan of action if we have to catch those crooks,' decided Sohrab. It was exactly what Appa and Altairbhai were thinking, of course. The children looked at each other—as if they hadn't thought of that. Why, they'd been making plans of action since they'd got to Lothal!

Appa was lost in thought, weighing up various options and their consequences.

The most important thing to do was to catch Uri and Hammur, redhanded, with the stolen treasures from the temple. How could they do that when they didn't have the right piece of the scroll to put together?

'I know, we have to give the real scroll to them,' he said finally. 'Then they will figure out the place, after joining the two parts. They will rush to dig there, and we shall follow them.'

'But,' he continued, pressing his nose hard, as he thought of the consequences, 'how should we do that? How can we lead them to the real package which you children have put in the well?'

'I know, Appa,' exclaimed Xerxes in high excitement. 'I'll get the package out. Amu here is still bruised, so it should be Kartik and me. We will keep it in the verandah. But someone has to tell Uri its there. How should we manage that?'

Kartik came up with the finishing touches. 'The men are sure to return after some time, as they will realize the map they have is false. They will go to Sohrab and ask him about the right map, which he will give to them this time. The girls should pretend to look for us boys and bump into them. The men will be sure to try and frighten them into revealing where our end of the map is and they will tell them. They won't check whether we are upstairs or not, they are sure to want to rush off to the correct place.'

'Yes, and then, we will follow Hammur and Uri and catch them redhanded,' suggested Appa.

'Look Kavi, can you be very brave? We will always be close to you, even if you can't see us. I feel they will soon be here,' said Xerxes, after conferring with Sohrab and Appa. Then he quickly outlined the plan he had in mind.

The only person who can go is Kavi,' reasoned Namami, looking terribly worried, as she told Appa again that the men would recognize her at once, and she was too petrified to even have them see her, forget about talking to them face to face. She had to be hidden as well as Kartik and Xerxes.

'Appa, please, please let me go,' pleaded Kaveri, wanting to be allowed to do her part for once.

'No, Kavi, these men are dangerous. You can't go,' said Appa very firmly.

'Appa, that is the best plan,' Xerxes intervened. 'See Kavi this is what you have to do, Appa, just hear this, and I'll be off. You go with Joker, meet the men in the courtyard and ask where we boys are. Then tell them we threw away the bag in the garden of the dried up well, and lead them there.'

Altairbhai laughed a little at how confident and independent the children had become, also seeing that their plan made sense. He convinced Appa, and at last their plan of action was decided upon.

'I was supposed to take back that parcel to Kadirbhai, to keep for Debuda,' said Sohrab, slowly considering other alternatives. 'I wish I knew the other half of the map they had earlier.

I'd have put it together and found the exact spot.'

'Well, sir I can draw it for you,' said Kartik quickly.

'Yes,' agreed the others, 'Kartik can draw very accurately and remembers everything,'said K averi. 'He's drawn it once and Amu has it.'

'We will, Kavi, in just a moment,' said Kartik soothingly. But other important things had to be decided first. As soon as all plans were clear, Xerxes would be off.

Quickly he drew an accurate map, from memory. Sohrab at once pulled the real map out from under his girdle, and they put it on the ground.

All of them studied it, keeping an ear open for Joker—he would bark if the thieves approached, they knew.

'Oh, it is so easy when it is put together!' exclaimed Xerxes, Namami, and Kartik together, and Kaveri too nodded her head. It was an exact picture of the maidan!

'We found bits of a seal, and the chief artisan told us what the carving was—a Pashupati, sitting under a peepul tree. And see, here is a peepul tree. This is the exact spot,' explained Kartik.

They had passed through that maidan a hundred times and knew every part so well. The two maps side-by-side gave the exact location of the peepul tree, and they could visualize the spot, pinpointed on the map with a cross. Some rishi must have meditated there sometime, and this is what the seal had shown. So Kartik's hunch had been right, the bits of the seal had been the most important clue!

The other symbols all made sense now: only if the moon shone bright, could you see the glimmering water! The boats too, could be seen from there, lying moored on a landing stage, during the day when the sun was shinning! And there were only peepul trees there. Four to be precise! The position of the hills, the snout shaped rock—the whole landscape fell into place now. If they had seen the cross without the seal clue, they would not have known the position of the tree. 'But how will they know they have to look under the peepul tree?' questioned Xerxes.

'I know!' exclaimed Namami. 'Kartik, you can somehow draw a peepul tree where the cross is, otherwise they will take so long to find it!'

Kartik ran out and soon came back, a wide grin on his face. 'I've found just the thing to draw with, it's a bit of red, unbaked brick. I'll be able to pinpoint the peepul tree. Let me just draw peepul leaves near the cross, they will understand.'

And he did exactly that, in record time. Now the trap had been set!

The two set off, quietly to the house with the dried well. They would find it easily enough. After all, they had just mapped out an entire campaign against the thieves who had dared to rob the sacred treasures of Mohenjo-daro!

The others decided to lie in wait for the men.

'I think we should tie you up again and leave you where they left you, Sohrabbhai and we should hide, atleast Kavi and me in the garden. When they come inside, Kavi you go to the courtyard with questions for them. I'll be right behind you, so that way, I am not worried,' decided Appa suddenly. 'They don't know we are here.'

They rushed inside and hurriedly picked up the longest cords and tied up Sohrab the way they had found him, but slightly looser, and wound the scarf around his mouth.

Then they went to the garden, and Appa, Amu, and Altairbhai found a place close to the gate, near a spreading shrub, and hid there.

Joker began to set up a great, big barking. It was time.

A Trap is laid

'Bow, wow wow,' barked Joker suddenly. He started growling as well! Kaveri went out into the courtyard, feigning innocence, and quaking a little inwardly. She was ready to play her part, but wasn't sure how well she could do it.

Uri and Hammur were there, looking angry and impatient.

'Look who's here!' Uri whispered to Hammur. 'Hey little girl,' he called out to Kaveri. 'We have been looking for you. We know you because of your dog. Weren't you on the elephant? Where is your friend?' Uri asked, with a large, false smile. Kaveri looked at the men boldly, although her heart was beating fast. Ignoring Uri's question she said politely, 'Please, sir, you've been walking here. Have you seen two boys, my brothers? We are looking for them.'

Uri and Hammur gave each other a quick look. So, were the boys really playing?

'No, little girl, but you have my parcel. My friend was on the elephant with you and he told me to ask you for it. You took his bag by mistake.'

'Oh, yes, we guessed that is what happened!' exclaimed Kaveri. 'Where is he? We looked for him, but couldn't see him anywhere.' She pretended not to know Hammur, as he had changed his clothes and was disguised as a hill person now. She continued, 'So we just threw it out.'

'Threw it oo—uuu—t-ttt?' screeched Hammur, his eyes almost popping out. Then he made himself say, in calmer tones,

'Where?'

Kaveri ignored his question, and said instead, 'I'm looking for my brothers, we are playing hide and seek; I think they might be in one of the houses here, they mentioned they were coming here this side. All of us came together. I am now going to the other house we were at before. Do you want to come? We left the bag there—should I show you?' She made a big, wide-eyed show of her innocence.

'Yes, yes, we will come, just wait for us here for a minute, and keep your dog with you. He's barking dangerously, and growling so much, can't you make him stop? What a noise, people will come here soon to see what the matter is.'

Kaveri had purposely pulled Joker's tail to make him bark the place down, of course!

The men ran into the burnt, abandoned house, in the meanwhile, and Kaveri smiled; she knew where they were going. Things were going according to the plan.

'Give us the other packet, you gave us the wrong one!' Uri shouted at Sohrab, trying to shake him. He hadn't realized that Sohrab had deliberately done this! Sohrab was pretended to be unconscious while the men searched him.

The men felt about Sohrab's robe, till they found the map, conveniently tucked inside the girdle of his robe. They left Sohrab, tied as he was and ran back out to Kaveri.

'Little girl, take us to the place where the parcel is. See, we have sweets in this bundle here for you.' said Hammur, with false sweetness. 'And really, can't you make that dog keep quiet!'

Kaveri quietened Joker. After all, his job—to bark loudly enough to make the men feel he was threatening and ready to attack—was done and she felt safe with him.

'He's very good, he bites anyone I tell him to... He looks after me, see how his fur is standing on end,' she said with a straight face. Let these horrid men feel scared, she thought. Joker was with her. She held on tight to his leash-rope. She wasn't scared now, well not *too* scared, anyhow. Her father was here. And the boys would be at the house nearby.

'It's a house with a dried well. Do you know it?' she questioned, again wide-eyed.

'Yes, we do, let's hurry and we'll be there soon,' the men replied. They walked briskly down the road and were soon at the other house. They had smiled at the few passers-by, impatient but not wanting to attract attention by running.

Meanwhile, Xerxes and Kartik had hastily brought the packet up from the well and put it out on the verandah. They were now inside the house, hiding.

Now, they lay in wait for the thieves, ready to execute the next step of their plan.

Outside, Uri and Hammur were walking through the courtyard. Kaveri walked behind them, at a safe distance. Joker was now quite silent. The sun's rays were long and low, and the shadows had lengthened; it was almost dusk, the sky a pale orange; a very mysterious time, thought Kaveri. Anything could happen.

And certainly she was proved to be right!

'Where can it be? Where did you put it, girl,' shouted Uri, his patience and sweetness at an end. They were being led on a wild goose chase through the garden. 'I don't remember... somewhere in the verandah,' Kaveri pretended to think, and finally told them. Sure enough they found it, the whole bundle with the map and that funny grey object which they hardly looked at but held onto, all the same.

Hammur and Uri sat down and put the maps together. Just like the children, they knew exactly where to look! Now they remembered what had been told to them.

'See, Uri, now we have the right section of the map, I can remember what Sonu told us!' exclaimed Hammur, with great delight.

'Sonu! Now WHO is Sonu?' thought Kaveri. Here is another lead, which I'll have to tell everyone about.

The men said a rough goodbye to Kaveri, hurrying away, and thinking to themselves what could a little girl do by herself? She wasn't likely to find the boys here, at any rate! Yes, *obviously*, she was quite in the dark as to what was happening.

They walked out of the courtyard as fast as they could, little knowing that a band of people was following them, at a safe distance, hiding in the trees and foliage on the side of the street.

Appa stepped out as soon as the men left. He had been barely a few feet away from Kaveri, on the sharp look out for any threat to her from Hammur and Uri. Right by him were the other boys, who had come out as soon as Uri and Hammur had left.

Namami was on the scene, as well, having found fresh, dark green aloe vera leaves, which she broke off, applying their sap to the boys' red, angry weals. Amu looked at Namami's hands. 'Healer's hands,' he thought, square and capable-looking, realizing again how lucky he was to have found these new friends of his.

The boys felt better. The burning sensation had reduced, and soon they were joking about it with each other, comparing it to the pain of bee stings.

Kaveri had waited for Altairbhai and Sohrab to come and join them; they in turn had been hiding just beyond the gate of the garden, waiting for the men to leave. As the group came together in the garden and followed Hammur and Uri, they didn't talk much. They kept pace with the thieves, maintaining the safe distance Altairbhai had decided on.

'We'll have to catch them in the act,' decided Appa, 'That is very important. Only then can they be taken to the tribunal of justice. Patiently they trailed the men for almost twenty minutes. The children decided to stop for a much needed drink of water at one of the public drinking wells. Uri and Hammur seemed to be so set on their mission; they didn't look back even once.

The children began to exchange news, and Amu looked at the tall, figure of Sohrab, who was hobbling now. Appa and Altairbhai noticed his increased weakness, and supported him on either side. He seemed familiar looking.

'Where have I met him?' Amu wondered. This was the first time he was seeing him up close, but the sun had set now and without flame torches everything, including faces and forms, looked indistinct and blurry.

'Sir, sir, pardon me, have we met before? In Morvinagar, or Mayurpur, or in Ranginapur? I feel

I've seen you before,' he asked Sohrab, politely, and hesitantly.

'No, my son—but again, my deeply grateful thanks for helping me, it was indeed brave of you. And you were tied up because of me. I will never forget it,' said the man, in his hoarse voice. The day's events had taken their toll on him.

He coughed again like he had when they had been held captive in that dark room, and once again Amu thought, 'I have seen him. I have heard just such a cough.' But try as he would, he could not remember.

Soon they found themselves near the maidan, and hid behind some boulders and bushes by the deserted path. Uri and Hammur had found the little group of trees, neem and peepul, and the banyan tree, close-by.

Most people were at the marketplace. The few who were around seemed deep in meditation, or were praying, totally absorbed. No one was paying any attention to them and apart from a few goats wandering around, it was fairly deserted.

The men looked at the map, did some calculations and marked off a part of it. They began digging. Khat, khat, dhad, dhad, khadaag, khadaag… They continued thus for at least ten minutes, sweating and cursing in the darkness, though there was some moonlight. They continued talking: there was no one to listen to them, they thought.

'It will be good to go back to Mesopotamia,' said Uri, who was struggling with the digging. Every few minutes there were some roots which had to be cut.

'It was a stupid idea of yours, Hammur, to doublecross Sonu... he would have led us here without all these problems. We should just have waited another week for him to come, then we would have divided the booty amongst us.'

'Then we'd have got less,' retorted Hammur sharply.

'We'll have to get the flame torches, I can't see anything now... Hammur, you go,' ordered Uri.

So Hammur hastily went to the market, right past the group who was watching him. Soon he was back with two torches on long sticks. 'I had to give my gold bead for both these, as they were already lit, and burning nicely,' he growled. Uri grunted and stuck the torches in the ground. Clearly this was no time to worry about a gold bead or two; they were on the brink of recovering the priceless treasures they had stolen, of many times that value. They had cleverly kept some of the precious necklaces and bracelets with them, in the sacks they carried on the elephant. But here were buried the temple articles, made of gold and silver, inlaid with precious stones.

The children began to feel as though they had pins and needles in their legs, but Appa cautioned them to stay still, as they watched the men continue to dig and listened on.

Hammur sat down after a while, feeling around with his hands in irritation. 'Are you sure this is the right place? I can't feel anything,' he hissed angrily. 'That Sonu! I hope what he told us about the hiding place was true, and he hasn't double-crossed us and hidden the temple treasures elsewhere.' They were lucky no one was there. The hillocks were ahead, on the eastern side, and it was in fact very lonely. No one used this area to cross the maidan because of the rocks and stones; one could stumble so easily, especially in the dark, though there was moonlight. They kept digging for another ten minutes, increasing the area and getting more tired and reckless in their speech.

'What a pity everyone started searching for the thief in Mohenjo-daro. But we left, with you disguised as a woman, ha!' said Hammur. 'Thank our fates that Sonu was ready to come here ahead, and bury this stuff while we pretended to search with the others! And it was good that Sonu gave Debuda all those messages. No one would ever suspect Debu of any wrongdoing. Now all we have to do is take all this back to Mesopotamia. How rich we'll be!'

'Hammur! I can feel something! Here!' Uri excitedly dug further and deeper, and then there was the sound of wood being hit.

'We've got it, Hammur! Our treasure! It's ours. We were so clever to give it to Sonu to hide. He will come soon, and we should be off to Mesopotamia before he arrives.'

'Stop chattering, you fool and continue digging till we get it out. We have to check that all we put in that sack is here, and that we have not been double-crossed.' Hammur wasn't ready to celebrate yet. His own crafty mind had planned the double-crossing of Sonu, in any case, when they got the first message to say he wasn't coming.

Then they pulled and heaved, and brought up two wooden boxes. They opened the bigger box. And there, in the darkness, with only the glow of the flames throwing light on them, glinted treasures the children had never imagined—necklaces of gold and silver; pearls and emeralds; jasper and jade and rubies, all glinting, shining; statues of gold; combs of gold and shell; amulets and charms; rings, bracelets, and anklets. The hidden people couldn't see very distinctly, but they could hear Hammur and Uri list everything greedily.

The thieves sat there, their hands deep in the treasure, looking on greedily, letting the jewellery slide gently through their hand. They were so enraptured that they were hardly aware of anything around them. There were the golden cups, gleaming dully, and the various vessels used during religious rites.

'Ours, ours! All ours! How clever we were to hit that guard and rob those gold statues. And these jewels! No one suspected us. And what about our first big robbery in Harappa? That nobleman was a fool, he showed us all the jewels he had! We stole some cunningly and quietly, slipping them into my bag while you talked, and he didn't check again! And told us about his friend who kept jewels in a pot under a floor, and how he was away! It gave us a clear field to steal everything there!' Uri gloated.

'When we reach Mesopotamia, we'll make sure we keep some aside, to be buried along with us, to take to the afterworld. As we get old, we will be asked what should be kept,' said Hammur, planning ahead.

'And what about our stay in Harappa—we took so many precious necklaces and rings, and gold ingots, and no one ever thought that two travelling vaids could get so friendly, and then take away their things. And how sorry we pretended to feel, and how we helped to look for everything, while keeping it safely with us! Ho ho ho!' chuckled Uri.

They carried on in this vein, full of vanity and pride in all their wrongdoing, and then they got the shock of their lives! For there, in the moonlight, stood Sohrab, whom they had left tied up. Behind him were two sturdy, hefty men and the boys they had held captive: an ambush they could never have expected!

Ever cunning, Uri and Hammur tried to escape. But they couldn't; they had the disadvantage of being in a squatting position, whilst digging. They thrashed around wildly, kicking and biting and hitting out blindly, but to no avail. Quickly, they were overpowered. Hands tied tight, they cursed vilely in Sumerian, shouting abuses at their captors.

But Appa put an end to all their struggles, abruptly. He told them sternly to be still and not to struggle. It was his voice that did it; cold as ice and full of contempt.

'We will take you with your stolen treasures to our priest-king. The council will decide what your punishment will be. You have done something terrible. You have robbed. You have cheated. You have been cruel and vicious with children—all unheard of here in peaceful Lothal. You have used violence. Now you will get a taste of Harappan justice!'

Altairbhai triumphantly produced the ropes he had kept for just this purpose, and with help from Sohrab, Appa, and the boys, bound the two men. They were then marched off by stern looking Altairbhai and grim Appa, both formidable, and the boys carried the two boxes between them. Finally, the treasures of Harappa would be returned to their rightful owners. Finally, justice and righteousness would triumph.

* * *

Amu prepared to leave as well, helping Sohrab pick up the torches. It was then that Amu, looking at Sohrab in the flickering light of the flames, suddenly remembered where he had seen him before.

It hit him like a bolt of lightning. His mouth went dry. He was speechless. It was crystal clear now.

'Sir—sir —please... ' he stammered, suddenly overcome with emotion.

'You are my father, oh, please say you are my father, sir,' Amu had caught hold of Sohrab's hands and was holding them tight, and beseeched him repeatedly to say that he was his father.

Sohrab turned a surprised face to Amu.

'Son, I am not your father. I have never set my eyes on you before. I am not married. I have no wife, nor any children. You are mistaken.' He silently pulled away from Amu's hands, which now held his arms in a vice-like grip.

'I wish that I was your father, such a brave lad like you, any father would be proud of,' he added gently, hearing sobs.

'Sir, sir,' Amu was sobbing loudly now, the pent up emotions of such a long and arduous quest finally overcoming him. It was as if a floodgate of emotions had been thrown open, and he couldn't stop weeping and talking, almost wildly.

'Father, my father, don't you remember me, your Amu, your life water, you used to say, more precious than anything else. You used to say I was just like you. See the amulet you gave me, see my neck and see the beautiful blue lapis lazuli. You have one too, my mother put it on for you before you set off on your travels to Mehluhaa, the same as mine, brought from the ravines of the Kokcha. It's a talisman to protect the wearer. Oh, say you are my father!'Cruel disappointment made his stomach curl.

Amu ran up to Appa, saying in a ragged voice, broken by sobs, 'Here is my father! Xerxes! Kartik! Nami, Kavi! See him, he never had a scar before, but it is him! It is his way of coughing, I know that cough!'

The children followed him, silent with pity, but at the same time hoping that this strange coincidence was indeed true, that Sohrab was in fact Amu's father.

Keeping their grip on the two criminals, Altairbhai and Appa turned, and listening to Amu felt a mixture of sympathy and joy. Appa knew that this was indeed something serious. The boy seemed so sure.

As they all proceeded, Sohrab, in his weakened condition, seemed to miss a step. Appa and Altairbhai shouted out, but it was too late. Sohrab had swayed, lurched, and fallen, unaware of the noise and commotion around him. The day's strain and this final news from Amu had overcome him. Appa sent Kartik to call ahead for help.

Amu wouldn't leave Sohrab, whose eyes were closed. He spoke of home, the rivers Tigris and Euphrates, the towns Nippur and Lagash and Ur, the ports, his brothers and sisters. He had found his father—though the sorrow and cruel irony was that his father did not know it. But whatever Sohrab said, Amu *knew* this was his father.

How could he not know his own father, his father who had told him tales of long ago, at whose knees he had learnt the song of Gilgamesh, just one of the many stories and adventures repeated at sunset?

Kartik returned with several townspeople whose kindly arms picked up Sohrab and took him to the small granary. Kindly hands also carried Amu away to rest. Beside himself with both grief and joy, he didn't seem to know what was happening.

So much had happened that the children could hardly take it in. The nobles arrived on the scene and their chief, who was always told of any emergency, or calamity, came as well. The chief priest-king was informed, and he too came hurrying; the other priest-kings were absorbed in prayer and could not be disturbed.

In a few minutes, ten men in charge of guarding the wrongdoers had arrived. Suddenly it felt like an army was out: everyone gathered to stare at this strange spectacle. Two grown men were being led, bound and defeated looking, by the guards and a group of tired yet victorious looking people.

Word spread fast and soon everyone knew what had happened. The men who had dared to steal the sacred treasures had been found, and would now be questioned. At last things would be set right.

Uri and Hammur had to answer to the chief priest-king, the same one who had told Amu not to lose hope. Appa and the boys, and even little Kaveri, and Namami were there, ready to listen to Hammur and Uri. It was Uri who spilled the beans. In fact, he squealed on Hammur! He wanted to save his own skin and be let off with a lighter punishment.

'We are from Mesopotamia, we had been travelling around, and thought we would settle here. But we had to work for our living! We learnt the local language and customs, but Hammur wanted to keep moving. That's how we stayed in Harappa and became friends with a nobleman, and later stole from him and his friend. Then we met Sonu, and became friends. But then we got tired of our hard life in Meluhha and decided to go back to Mesopotamia. Sonu said he too wanted to go with us, the life seemed easier there; there are no slaves in Meluhha. We told him one needed money to have a good life there: slaves and luxury cost money. The easy way for us was to steal. We had nothing to give in exchange for our passage back to Mesopotamia. We had to get worthy articles in exchange for the trip. We started with small thefts, then Hammur became bolder. Seeing this, Sonu told him about the temple treasures, saying there were many riches there. He decided that once we had a great amount of precious articles, we would go. So a plan was made, but only Hammur and I carried out the actual robbery. '

He paused and pointed at his partner. 'Yes! He was the one who planned them. He hit the guard of the temple,' Uri blubbered, and blurted out.

'After the robbery, the guards in Mohenjo-daro were looking for the thief with great urgency. They tried to follow all clues. It had become unsafe for us to stay there anymore. Sonu told us the quickest way was to go by sea, from Lothal, which he knew well. We divided the stolen goods, but we kept the more precious, smaller jewels as it would be safer for us. After all, people knew we were originally from elsewhere, and we were scared about temple treasures.

Sonu made a plan. He knew where it was safe to bury the treasure and he would do it. He drew a map and explained it to us but he didn't tell us all. He kept half the scroll and gave us one half, so that even if we were caught, or he was, no one would be able to locate the stolen stuff. We could get it later, he said. But he kept the map, with the exact spot marked with a cross, with him! He gave us the other part of the scroll.'

All of a sudden, Uri was interrupted by Hammur, who shouted at Uri in Sumerian language, and from the tone everyone could make out he was cursing him!

'But why were you carrying that waxy object?' asked Xerxes and Kartik and Appa, puzzled.

'Oh that Sonu told us to do. And he told us the names of Debu and Kadir. We have never met them before!'

'Then Hammur had the idea of running away with the treasure as Sonu would come later. "Let's desert him, we will have more money and enjoy life," he said.'

Everyone was listening open-mouthed. What kind of people were these? There was supposed to be honour among thieves as well!

There was an uproar, as Hammur tried to kick Uri, wild with anger. Then they were taken away, and locked up. There was so much excitement that everything seemed queer and make believe to the children.

Appa took over. 'You children, after all this, you need food and rest. I don't want to hear a word,' he announced with the authority only a father or mother has. The children were too tired to object.

He collected some food, and for once no one was aware of what they were eating. They gathered in the small granary and dropped off to sleep at once.

Even Joker was tired with all the bounding and barking and jumping he had done that day. He turned round and round, in his usual way, and finally fell sound asleep by Namami's side. After this, all was quiet except for the odd snore. No one, except poor, troubled Amu, stirred an inch. 'Go to sleep, Amu. Tomorrow will bring all the answers, pray to your gods now, and sleep,' Appa told him.

Amu prayed to Enki and Nannar, and Utu and Enlil, and the prayers were from his heart. 'Tomorrow, let my father know me.'

Sohrab's story

When Amu woke up, he was surprised to find the others awake, waiting for him to get up. He didn't know he had talked and talked in his sleep, tossing and turning, and muttering again and again. Appa had ended up watching over him, calming him gently and patting him to sleep. Even Joker had not been allowed to bark near him.

Amu looked around him and remembered Sohrab and the discovery of his real identity, and joy lit up his face. He felt bright and hopeful.

'He is my father,' he told them all with conviction in his voice. 'How he has forgotten me, I do not know. But now I am not dejected or sad. There is a way out of this maze, and I will find it.'

The fives had been ordered by Appa to bathe, change, and eat the chikoos, guavas, and nuts and sesame seed bread he had brought for them. And he had another set of clothes for them to change into, in his cart!

Appa congratulated them first, telling them how proud he was of all of them. The children looked at each other grinning, still unable to believe they had actually found the temple treasure.

'And you were wonderful, Kavi. So brave to go alone and talk to those thugs,' he told his youngest with pride. The others all clapped her on the back.

Kartik felt pride at having such a brave little girl for his sister and told her so. Kaveri beamed shyly, happy that although she had been scared, she had done as planned.

Now, Appa told them all he knew. Uri and Hammur were now awaiting justice. The priest-king had been given all the stolen objects and he was full of gratitude. He had come to Lothal to lead the prayers for the Surya Mela, with no inkling that he would take back the treasure discovered by the children. It was a great victory for him, and he could hold his head high again.

He had also explained the importance of the treasure to Appa. Some of it was precious necklaces, beads, bracelets, bangles, and hair combs stolen from various people.

The grey waxy object turned out to be the famous dancing girl! At this the children gasped. To think they had held it in their hands, and not known what it was. Why, they might even have left it anywhere!

Appa explained what he thought was the riddle of Sonu, the Harappan thief, giving the dancing girl to Uri and Hammur.

'If he had been caught redhanded with it, there would have been severe justice meted out to him. He had stolen a temple treasure, which concerned the honour of Mohenjo-daro and Harappa! He wanted to be innocent of that particular crime, if he was ever found out. Now, word has been sent quietly to where he is, and he will be apprehended and will come before the tribunal of justice.'

Yes, it had been the beautiful dancing girl statue in the package. The wax had been removed, then the layers of cloth, and then the dancing girl in all her glory was revealed with her hands on her hips, dancing innocently, wearing nothing but bangles right up to her arms. There were precious jewels at her neck, and jasper and jade ornaments adorned her hair, which was made up in an elaborate, old-fashioned style. There was a golden stick inserted through the gap between where her hand rested on the waist. The small gold stick had a gold harvest sheaf of wheat at its end, and was encrusted with precious gems and glittered and shone, now that it had been cleaned. It was a beautiful bronze figure, a real work of art.

This temple property would return to Mohenjo-daro, to be used for its rightful purpose—in devotion, not for personal gain, Appa concluded. The children sat back and sighed, realising that their adventure with the dancing girl, and the treasure that had accompanied her, was finally over.

Just then one of the priest-king's men came up shouting, 'A miracle! A miracle! I have the best news to give all who are here. Listen carefully.' He told them what had happened.

The priest-king had been to the doctor who was attending to Sohrab. The doctor had made a long face, sadly shaken his head, and said, 'I am afraid I cannot do anything for your friend. I had given him a medicine, a draught last night when I was watching him. That is all I can do. We will have to wait and watch now.'

No sooner had the words been uttered than Sohrab woke, muttering feverishly, 'Where am I? What has happened to me, what am I doing here?' He then dropped off into a deep sleep and woke up an hour later, looking much better.

'I remember now! That fall must have knocked me senseless, but it was a blessing in disguise, for it has opened the pathway to my old memory and poured light on the darkness of my past,' Sohrab had reportedly told the priest-king. 'I was so ashamed. I could remember nothing of my past. Was I a criminal on the run? Was I exiled from somewhere? I pretended to know my past, always fearful I would meet someone who may say I was not a good man. Call my son! Yes yes! I do remember him!'

The priest-king had then told him of Amu's sacred quest, the one which had been revealed to him, and things fell into place.

Appa looked at Amu and smiled. 'Let us go meet your father,' he told the boy. Amu grinned, and everyone rushed out at once to the doctor's house, to reunite Amu with his long lost father.

There was an emotional meeting between Amu and his father. Amazement, wonder, joy, and sorrow too—these expressions were there for all to see, in a little room in the small granary, which had been made into a doctor's room.

Amu's father had his arm around him, and held him tight, as if never to lose him again. There was much talk of the family—Amu's mother, the children—and both father and son wept unashamedly this time.

'How my mother will rejoice!' cried Amu joyously. There was a prayer of thanksgiving by all, and Appa presided over it solemnly.

There were so many explanations awaited still, and hundreds of questions, and finally Sohrab told his story.

Everyone sat around him, eager to hear all he had to say.

He had been travelling alone, having told the captain of the ship in which he had come that he would return on another ship. On his travels, he had fallen from a cliff top and had lain unconscious and lost his memory. 'I was picked up by kindly villagers... My head wound was very bad. They didn't even know if I would live, I was so weak, and I had such a high fever. They put herbal pastes and poultices, hour after hour, made me brews, and nursed me back to health.'

'For some days I felt an emptiness I could not fathom. When I recovered enough to move around, I left and wandered for months, not understanding much. I had completely forgotten my past. I worked in the fields, sometimes I picked fruit in fruit orchards. I went from clan to clan, I went as far as Harappa.'

'Harappa! Do you mean to say Harappa, which is on the banks of the river Ravi? That is very far away!' exclaimed Altairbhai, in astonishment.

Sohrab nodded, looking up with a bright, open expression, and continued, 'Then I went to Mohenjo-daro. I went to the long, low wooden temple spread over much land, and a sense of peace came upon me.

'I had a purification bath in the Big Bath there. It is a grand ritual. Every day so many people enter and the water is kept clean and fresh.

'I saw the priests' college and the long hall with its many pillars, and I was reminded of something; I knew not what, nor where my memory was seeking answers. I saw the fire altar and the beautiful bowls with the sacred borders of peepul leaves. They were full of offerings of fruit, flowers, grain, vegetables, and day and night there was the fragrance of camphor and incense burning in the sacred brazier.'

'Wandering around, I became a nomad, never staying long enough to know any one. Except for Debuda and Kadirbhai and a few other people, I had no family or friends. But Kadirbhai called me his brother, and so did Debuda, so they became my family.'

'I lived my day to day life working so hard that I would fall asleep and forget what the day told me: that actually I didn't know who I was. Soon I started to feel like a part of Mehluhha. As it is, there are so many different races living in harmony here; the hill tribes and river tribes, and tribes who live deep in the jungles. At first, I used to wonder about my past, but decided I was alone as no one had tried to find me, or made any enquiries. I had no memory of a family so I convinced myself that I had none. Surely I would remember some names or have some vague blurry idea of a wife and children, I thought. But no, there was a vacuum. So I just put my faith in the spirits and lived as though I was born here.

'I had decided to stay at Dholavira, that was one name that stayed in my mind, the village where I had been nursed back to life. I wanted to find the people who looked after me and saved my life.'

'I planned to come to the Surya Mela to pray for my memory, or if not, to find some peace. Debuda was given the package by someone, but couldn't come with me. Then, Kadirbhai was going to come with me, but his old father fell sick. Finally, I was the only one coming here. Hence it was given to me, with instructions about taking the parcel in return. I suppose whoever gave the parcel to Debuda knew what the grey waxy object was, and planned to keep it.'

The four children said at once, 'Oh, that must have been Sonu who gave that. We know

now. All has been made clear!' And the five laughed happily.

'So it's true, too many thieves and the loot vanishes: one double-crosses the other!' laughed Appa.

Xerxes had one question. 'Sir, where is your blue stone amulet? Whenever you looked at it, didn't it remind you of your family?'

'No, my son, I no longer have it. It may have broken off and fallen when I had my first fall, or maybe someone stole it. I will never know,' he replied with a wry smile.

The priest-king came then, and there was a solemn ceremony of gratitude for the great kindness shown to them by the gods Enki, Enlil, An, and Etu.

Everyone was happy. The priest-king said solemnly, 'This is the day of the holy Surya Mela. It is auspicious, see the proof. That boy came from across the seas, and the alignment of the planets—the sun at the right place over the confluence at the moment of its zenith—everything came together. The spirits of all the powers blessed him and helped to reunite with his father, and the white parrot of his land gave him hope. And the temple treasures have been returned. For that too, I am thankful.'

Surya Mela

The great day of the Surya Mela finally arrived. The early morning sky was a rosy pink, with little white clouds scudding across it. The air was cool and there was a sense of serenity all around. The birds too seemed to know this, for there were many different kinds flying about, or sitting on low branches, whistling softly, their long, true notes filling the quiet morning sky. Yes, this was the day of the Surya Mela when all planets would be in alignment. Two days earlier, the children had proudly shown Amu the constellations they knew, and now the auspicious time had come.

Everyone was happy. It was a day for counting blessings and making offerings. The children had been plied with thanks and prayers by grateful people for solving the mystery of the missing temple treasure. What was more, the priest-kings had decided that the children would help when the prayers started: a signal honour for them, and a memory to be treasured all their lives.

Amu too was to participate in the formal rites, as decreed by the chief priest-king. After all, the elements—sun, water, wind, earth—were universally worshipped. The spirits were all the same, despite being called by different names in different lands. Amu was overwhelmed by this honour. This was another amazing story to be told to everyone at home!

They all collected at the sangam of the Aravalli and the Pavitra rivers. Appa watched his children with pride.

He was pleased with the change he saw in them. Kartik, who was shy and hesitant at times, had become bolder and more practical. He had grown up now!

Xerxes was less impatient and more constructive in his thinking; not dreaming only about the sea, but taking on responsibility like a man. Namami remained the same—wise and loving—with her sense of fun intact; but the timidity seemed to have vanished as well as the nervousness she had sometimes showed, earlier.

And Kaveri, though still the youngest, had gained in stature, ready to take her place as a part of the group. After all, she had been a key player in leading Hammur and Uri to the treasure, and ultimately catching them. Yes, Appa was proud of all the children!

Joker was praised and fussed about for his role, and he barked happily, looking as though he was laughing. He loved the attention! He too had played a big part in all of this, and he knew it.

They all chanted now, along with others:

'We salute you, O Spirit of the Sun

Hear us, O giver of life
One who bestows all life force
One who nurtures our soul and our spirit
Giver of light, Healer
Protector of righteousness
Grant us some of your energy
Ensure that the darkness of evil never enters our soul
Sun, manifestation of the whole universe
O, one who controls the animate and inanimate
Sun, soul of the universe
Grant us wisdom and courage and peace

Amu watched, spellbound. He couldn't wait to describe this to everyone at home.

A boat was leaving for Mesopotamia after seven days. Sohrab was impatient to leave, but promised to return. And in these seven days Amu was to collect gifts to take home, including two monkeys! Shyon with Binku, the monkey, had been present in the crowd, and he and his clan were so happy for Amu. Shyon knew a person who had some tamed monkeys, and he told Amu that as long as he looked after them well, he could have them.

Kaveri hung around Amu, for she had got really attached to him. Giving him a sweet smile, she held his big hand in hers and said, 'Amu, promise you will visit us again? Just promise!' And Amu laughed, pulling her long plaits, saying he would!

Then the real business of bartering, exchanging, and carrying presents began for all of them.

Carnelian necklaces for Amu's sisters; shining faience toys, made of powered quartz sand and other materials, which glinted like metal; fine muslin... the list was endless. The generous people at the Surya Mela had loaded them with all kinds of gifts and wares. Xerxes would take back shinning faience squirrels and rams for the young ones at home, and copper bangles or maybe a bronze bordered framed mirror for his shy, quiet mother. He felt thankful he hadn't been foolish enough to trade his valuable coat; now he knew he would have regretted it. Amu played happily with all the children, the cloak of responsibility he had always worn sliding off him: he was just a regular thirteen year old boy now.

Soon the mela closed. They all had had a wonderful time, laughing, playing, but all underlaid with a little sadness, as they knew it would be some time before they could all meet again, except for Xerxes, who was sure he would sail to far off lands!

A note on place names

Mesopotamia: The name of an ancient civilization found in modern day Iraq and part of Syria, mainly between the rivers Euphrates and Tigres.

Meluhha: The ancient name given to India, by people from Mesopotamia.

Lagash, Ur, Kish, Umma, Nippur: Sumerian city-states in ancient Mesopotamia.

Dilmun: The old name for Bahrain and Failaka islands, located in the Persian Gulf.

Sutkagen dor: A port on the Makran coast of Pakistan, on the river Dasht.

Avaganaa: An ancient name for Afghanistan.

Meghrgarh and Amri: Cities in modern day Pakistan.

Lothal, Dholavira, Akhnoor: Present day Indian towns and villages, which still have people living and farming there. These are local names, which have been passed down orally over the years.

Anantpur, Namaksagar, Neelamabad, Kuntasini, Bansiwali, Ranginapur, Roparrani: Fictitious names for villages and settlements in present day Gujarat.

A note on the dancing girl statue

Of all the ancient artifacts belonging to the Indus Valley Civilization, perhaps the most interesting is the statue of the dancing girl. The 4500 year old bronze statue was discovered by the fireplace of a ruined house in Mohenjo-daro, in 1926. About ten centimeters high, the statue is of girl in a dancing pose with one hand on the hip, and the other resting on the thigh, adorned in bangles all the way up her arm. Around her neck is a necklace with three large pendant-like beads. Her hair is coiled in an elaborate bun. The statue shows superb craftsmanship and skill. It was cast by an advanced technique for shaping metal known as the lost-wax process, which is used till today. Some archeologists think that the statue could well be of a queen or some other important woman in the life of Mohenjo-daro, judging by the authority the figure commands.

Acknowledgements

Special thanks to Priya and Gaurav, who helped so much, and gave the first 'thumbs up'. This book wouldn't have been written without them, and without their knowledge of recalcitrant computers! Thanks to Arjun and Ashwini for all their support, and little Diya for her laughter. Thanks also to my enthusiastic sister Kanchan, who encourages me, as do my sisters Savita, Nayana, my sister-in-law, Nileem, and the larger family. And most of all, thanks to my mother, who feels very thrilled to see my name in print! Niteen, who has always given me time to do anything, gets a very special thank you. Thank you to Ishan Khosla for designing a really beautiful cover. Finally, Neyata, Rajni, and Chiki—my editors, who did a wonderful job asking me questions, which I HAD to answer; I learnt a lot in the process. A big thank you to them.

A note on the author

Sunila Gupte is the author of two children's books, *From Pumpkins to Pickles* and *Quest for the Quetzal Feather*. Her short stories for children have frequently featured in *The Hindu* and *Deccan Herald*, and she has written for *The Indian Express*, *Sanctuary Cub* and *Children's World*. Sunila has taught English and French for many years, and has worked for *The Times of India's* Newspaper in Education (NIE). Currently, she lives in Bangalore.